Straight Arrow

Straight Arrow

A.J. Schuster

Copyright © 2008 by A.J. Schuster.

Library of Congress Control Number:		2008902529
ISBN:	Hardcover	978-1-4363-0856-4
	Softcover	978-1-4363-0855-7

All rights reserved. No part of this book may be reproduced or transmitted in any form or by any means, electronic or mechanical, including photocopying, recording, or by any information storage and retrieval system, without permission in writing from the copyright owner.

All characters in this novel are fictitious.

This book was printed in the United States of America.

To order additional copies of this book, contact:
Xlibris Corporation
1-888-795-4274
www.Xlibris.com
Orders@Xlibris.com
40239

Chapter 1

"God damn it, Mr. President, you've got to do something. Every bozo in politics is ahead of you in the polls. About the only one who's trailing is Wendell Willkie."

The PR man started and opened his eyes. "I thought he died."

The president tried to impale his chief aide with his weak blue eyes. "I am not going to be the president who brought back rationing. And price controls are out of the question. The American people are starting to conserve oil—."

"Yeah," interrupted the chief aide. "By the time the world's oil supply runs out, they'll be down to a mere million barrels a day."

The secretary of defense clasped his hands over his paunch. "The Ayatollah gave us the perfect excuse for taking over Iran and its oil wells when he took those hostages. If we had acted promptly and decisively, as I suggested—."

"The Russians would have loved that," put in the aide.

"So?" asked the defense secretary. "They seem to love everything else we do."

"Hey, talking about Iran," said the PR man, leaning forward. "Did you see that cartoon in the paper yesterday? Uncle Sam is drilling a hole through the earth, and it comes up under Iran. Sucks the whole place dry!"

The president looked pained as his PR man chuckled. The secretary of energy stopped drumming his fingers on his chair arm and gazed at the man.

"Hell, George, don't look so serious." The PR man was enjoying himself. "Everybody knows if you dig a hole all the way through the earth, you'll come out in China." He roared with laughter.

The secretary glanced at his deputy, who nodded.

"Actually, the technology's there," said the deputy. "Lasers, what have you. But you'd need someone who could—." The president was staring open-mouthed, and his aide had a glazed look.

"There was a guy once," continued the deputy, "who could have done it."

"What happened to him?" asked the secretary.

"Got pissed at his girlfriend. I think he's in prison in New Mexico . . . for about one hundred and ten years."

The president closed his eyes. "Isn't there someone else who could handle this?"

"I don't know of anyone," said the deputy, "who has the background and the skills this man has. He's worked in oil drilling and he developed a laser for deep underground work."

"And we know he's crazy," remarked the chief aide. "That's another criterion for this project."

The deputy turned to him. "He was very well respected in his field, before he took up with that . . . woman . . . and lost his head."

"Assuming we could get the services of this man," said the chief aide, "just where would you drill from? Staten Island? And how do you explain things to Russia, and the UN . . . not to mention Iran?"

The deputy spread his hands. "You could set up operations anywhere . . . in a jungle in Central America, if you like. No one would detect the drilling itself unless he were specifically looking for it."

"The CIA could be brought in, to assure secrecy," said the defense secretary. "Now that Congress has taken off those ridiculous restraints against covert activities . . . ."

"I suppose the president could grant the man a pardon," suggested the energy secretary.

His deputy frowned. "I think that might be difficult. It was a particularly unpleasant murder."

"Well," said the chief aide, "we could always send the CIA into the prison yard in a helicopter, and waft him away into the blue yonder." The conversation was getting out of hand, but he took the opportunity to smile sweetly at the defense secretary.

The president got to his feet. Was this a joke, or was this a joke?

"I have a prayer meeting to attend, gentlemen." He rested his hand on the defense secretary's shoulder for an instant, as he moved toward the door. "Arthur, I know I can trust you to see that any plan that evolves will be in full accord with the laws of the land . . . or some reasonable facsimile thereof."

The energy secretary turned to the secretary of defense as the door closed.

"Perhaps we should send someone to New Mexico to do a preliminary study."

The PR man jumped up. "I'll find out about visas and shots right away."

Chapter 2

J.B. Craddock took a hard pull at the straw and watched the last bubbles rise from the paper cup. No matter how hard he fantasized, it still tasted like soda pop. "God damn," he muttered, "I haven't had a shot of sour mash in three years."

He jumped at the touch of a hand on his shoulder. "You got a visitor, J.B.," said the guard.

"You're crazy, I don't know anybody."

"Too bad," the guard leered. "I wouldn't mind having a visitor looked like her."

J.B. furrowed his brow as he followed the guard out of the dining room and down the corridor. His sister Ruth had never answered his letters. Cousin Janie was living over in Louisiana, and Marybelle—well, that was the reason he was here, wasn't it.

The clang of a gate roused him. They stepped into the tiny intersection in front of the guard's station. The guard rapped on the second gate, heard the buzzer, and swung it open. They stepped into another corridor.

Buzz, clang. Buzz, clang. He had measured his life in buzzes and clangs for the past three years. He had become accustomed to the expressionless eyes of the guards watching him, to the paper plates and plastic knives and forks, even to sleeping with five men in a barred cubbyhole. But somehow he had never been able to push the buzzes and clangs beneath his consciousness.

"Spread 'em."

"What? Oh." He spread his arms and legs. He peered through the window of the visitors' room to take his mind off the stubby fingers crawling down his sides and up his legs, around his crotch. This better be worth it, he thought.

A guard pointed him to a table, and she stood up to meet him. Red hair pulled back with a scarf, brown mascaraed eyes, about a size eight, with nice curves here and there.

"J.B., it's been so long," she whispered with a slight lisp, "kiss me." They leaned forward over the table. He felt her tongue probing for his. His legs were weak. Three years. Hell, that wasn't her tongue. She drew back slowly, eyes glistening with love. He sank down into the chair.

"Just listen," she said. The lisp was gone. "I'm a federal agent. We need your particular skills for an operation of vital importance to this country. If you work with us, you can forget about this place. Just nod if we can count on you."

He nodded.

"You now have the means to get out of here. Arrange to have some others go with you—decoys. At seven o'clock on the evening of April tenth the fence wires on the southeast perimeter of the yard will be cut. Straight down from Building C. I'll be waiting for you on the bridge two miles north of here. If you're not there by eight o'clock, we'll assume you've changed your mind. Are you with me?"

He nodded again, trying to file away what she was saying, to absorb it. Questions kept getting in the way. But he knew they had little time.

"One thing," he said carefully.

"Yes?"

"Don't suppose you could get me some sour mash before that."

"Oh. Of course." She leaned forward again, touching his cheek gently, pulling his head down.

He saw the white curve of skin, the beige bra, and struggled to keep from gulping. Three years. Goddam! There was a straw sticking out of the bra. He leaned down, nuzzling her flesh, moving the cylinder to one side of his mouth. Then he sipped. He closed his eyes. Sour mash. When he finally came up for air, he was smiling.

"Lady," he said, "you've got a date."

"Spread 'em," said the guard, at the door to the corridor. He was watching the redhead swinging her hips as she walked to the visitors' door, and patted down J.B. perfunctorily.

"Muy bonita," he said, as J.B. turned down the corridor. "You think she'll wait for you, man?" He laughed gleefully. J.B. smiled back at him.

Chapter 3

"So like I said, where do we put this operation? Staten Island?"

"Why are you always so negative?" the PR man asked.

"I don't believe in trying to fool Mother Nature," the chief aide responded, leaning back in his chair. "I just flow with the river of life."

"I can't believe that guy got you elected, Mr. President," huffed the PR man.

"It sure as hell wasn't you, Rebecca of Sunnybrook Farm."

"Gentlemen," sighed the president, "let us reason together."

"Reason flew out the window," retorted the aide, "when these kooks proposed their cockamamie scheme."

The secretary of energy drummed his fingers on his chair arm. "As we have said, Mr. President, the technology is there. Personally, I feel the present crisis calls for a bold stroke, some dynamic action."

"Personally," said the chief aide, "I've always preferred dynamic inaction. But I'm democratic. I'll go with the majority."

"I vote for Panama," said the PR man. "We've got the canal right there, we can ship the oil up—."

The president winced. "The Panama Canal," he explained, "no longer belongs to us."

"And why bother with shipping?" asked the deputy secretary of energy. "Surely there must be some place in the U.S. where we'd attract no attention . . . one of those big states out West, with a small population . . . ."

"They're still mad at us for trying to make them the garbage dump of the nuclear power industry," said the chief aide.

"They don't vote for us anyway," observed the president. "And we own most of the land."

"White Sands," announced the defense secretary, thumping the president's desk. "There's no one out there, and it's closed to visitors."

The PR man coughed. "Isn't that where we exploded the first A-bomb?"

"That's the place," nodded the defense secretary.

"Isn't it, ah, dangerous? The radioactivity?"

The defense secretary laughed. "Don't be silly. That was almost fifty years ago."

"You know, I think you've got something," the chief aide admitted. "Nobody's going to think anything of oil coming out of New Mexico. It's one of the biggest domestic producers now."

"Our man in New Mexico might not like being so close to home," the PR man ventured.

"That's his problem," snapped the aide. "We're breaking him out, aren't we?"

The president winced again. "Arthur," he said, turning to the defense secretary, "you're in charge of this operation, since White Sands is a military installation." He nodded toward his aide. "Sam will represent the interests of the White House. Unofficially, of course."

Chapter 4

"Craddock! What in hell you doing?"

"Blast you!" J.B. hissed. "Shut your face and get over here."

J.B. hadn't expected any of his cellmates to return so soon. No one ever rushed back to his cell from the dining room, but J.B. had, to try out his little present.

It was a skinny sectioned piece of plastic that opened out into an eight-inch saw blade. No wonder the metal detector hadn't caught her. The blade was edged with diamond dust.

And it was cutting very nicely into a steel bar that marred the view from his cell window.

"Jésus y Maria," Chongo breathed, glancing back toward the corridor. It was empty. "When you going out, man?"

"Couple of weeks. When the time looks right."

"You take me with you, man. I know this town. I can help you."

"OK, but cool it. Just keep an eye on the guard."

Eventually, of course, he took them all in. They were a mangy lot, he thought. If decoys were needed, they'd do in a pinch.

There was Ernesto Rodriguez, who, fancying himself a redeemer of his oppressed people, called himself, after his famous namesake, Ché. His revolutionary activities had consisted mainly of petty thefts until, angered by the measly twelve dollars and fifty-three cents proffered by a victim, he had bashed in the man's head with the butt of a gun.

Tranquilino Gonzales had been muy tranquilino ever since his first fix of heroin at the age of sixteen.

Wild Bill Everett had ridden his motorcycle into the lobby of a prestigious hotel on the first night of Santa Fe's fiesta. When the police checked his fingerprints, they found he was wanted for rape in three states.

Sammy Sloane had raped a teacher in a schoolyard, and then strangled her.

Then there was Chongo, Alfonso Martinez, whose dreams of glory were inspired by nothing more potent than marijuana. Unfortunately, he liked to share the good times, and had tried to share with a narc.

And there was J.B. Craddock. Whatever had happened to the unwritten code about a crime of passion, he mourned, killing an unfaithful sweetheart in the hot flood of anger and agony?

*   *   *

For three weeks J.B. sawed and pondered, sawed and schemed. What skill of his was it that the government needed so desperately? He had been a bush pilot in South America once, flying in and out of fields the size of a postage stamp carved out of vertical walls of the Andes. Once, in La Paz, he remembered—. Hell, no, there were lots of pilots on the outside who could do that.

He had tried selling insurance for a while.

Maybe they needed a killer who could be counted on not to talk later. No, the government had plenty of those, too.

What would happen to him after he did what they wanted? Would they set him up with a new identity, or pardon him—or ship him back to prison? He'd have to get that settled right off.

He thought of the days drilling for oil in West Texas. Those were good times. Stinking, dirty, grinding work, and then, when the money flowed, raising hell in every Lone Star Saloon on both sides of the Mexican border. Well, there were lots of people who could find oil. The government didn't need him for that. He had experimented after that with—.

"Hey!"

He jumped. Chongo had put down his newspaper and was looking at him.

"Hey, J.B., you been reading about this guy, the Ayatollah? What a prick. Man, we should of just sent in the marines, you know? Would have had all that oil, too."

Oh, no, J.B. thought, they wouldn't. They'd have to be out of their fucking minds. Oh, no.

* * *

"Hey, J.B., when are we going?"

"Shut up and read your comic book, Sammy." They were in the library, and J.B. was trying to look out the window nonchalantly at the guard tower.

"But you haven't told us a thing," Sammy whined. "When you going to give us the plan?"

"When I'm ready," J.B. answered.

"How do we know we can trust you?" Sammy narrowed his eyes.

J.B. glanced at him with distaste. "If you don't think you can trust me, stay out of it. You don't have to go."

"Well, but—how do you know you can trust those friends of yours? What if we get out in the yard and the guards just gun us down?"

"Easy come, easy go, Sammy."

J.B. got up and went to check out a book. He was wondering about his friends, too.

Chapter 5

April tenth was a Sunday. Perfect for an escape. It was a visiting day, and inmates came and went unescorted through the corridors. The guards were hungover or nonexistent. Sunday was a favorite time for calling in sick.

Chongo watched him staring out the cell window. "When are we going, J.B.?" he asked quietly.

"Tonight. After dinner call."

The others clambered out of their bunks and crowded around him. "Is everything all set?" "Are you sure we're ready?"

"No problem. Now don't be so subtle. Get out and move around."

They had trouble keeping from bumping into one another during the day. Ché and Wild Bill developed a thirst for literature and scoured the library shelves, sending furtive glances toward J.B. Craddock lounged in a chair reading *Historic Sites of Old New Mexico*, which contained a fine map of the area in which the prison was located. Of course, he had no idea where the redhead was going to take him. Maybe she wouldn't show. Or maybe he would ditch her and try to get to Mexico. He studied the roads to keep himself from thinking about all the maybe's.

Chongo almost got into a fight with a guard who reminded him the barbershop was closed on Sunday, and what was the big hurry, anyway. "They been after you to cut your hair for months, Chongo, why you suddenly need a haircut today? Your mama coming to visit you?" He laughed and strolled away.

They finished dinner quickly—a fringe of meat clinging to a big round ham bone, a baked potato that tortured the flimsy plastic forks. Then they hurried back to the cell block. Officer Lucero opened the last gate—buzz, clang—and watched them enter their cell.

"Have a good meal, boys?" he asked. But he had already turned back toward the guard's station, to labor over the endless reports.

"It was terrific," called Chongo. "Steak and french fries."

He stood, stretching lazily, at the grill gate, while J.B. gently pulled out the section of bars he had sawed through. Four of them went through the window. J.B. waved to Chongo, then followed. Chongo yawned and started humming.

Hunched over, J.B. led them along the back wall of the cell block. He stopped at the corner and stood up. The night air smelled clean and sweet, with a hint of piñon. He wondered who the guard was up in the tower. It didn't matter much. They all got snowblind after a while. But he hoped it wasn't Delaney. Delaney would love to shoot an inmate's ass.

"Don't run," he whispered, "just straight ahead." He pushed them out one by one into the grassy yard, spacing them a few seconds apart. He took a deep breath and followed, crouching like an ape.

It was absolutely quiet except for the thud of their feet. Everyone in the pen must hear us, he thought.

They were huddled along the first fence, shadowed by the roll of concertina wire along the top edge.

"J.B., I don't see—."

"Shut up," he growled. He moved along the fence, pressing gently.

Goddam it, where was it? Five feet . . . ten. A thud behind him brought him up straight and he whirled. Chongo smiled and gave him a thumb's up sign.

Five feet more. The wire separated, stinging his hand. He bent back the flap easily. Right behind it, he found the cut in the second fence. He led them out a few hundred feet.

"OK," he whispered, "you're on your own. Just take it easy until you're off the grounds."

Chongo hesitated. "J.B., you don't want to come with me? I can help you, bro'. I know this town."

"We've got a better chance if we separate, Chongo." J.B. squeezed his shoulder. "Cuidate."

"Yeah, you take care, too, man." He turned and moved away.

J.B. watched the shadows creep away. A couple of them stayed together. The others spread out in different directions, each with his own vision of freedom. He waited ten minutes. He wasn't going to take anybody with him.

He walked in the ditch along the road, recoiling when he brushed against the dry weeds. No cars passed. Everybody home on Sunday watching television.

The bridge was just ahead. He slowed. Nothing. Where was she? Don't panic. She's got it timed just right. Carefully, he parted the weeds at the far side of the bridge and crawled in and lay down. And waited.

Chapter 6

"Man, ain't you glad I came along when I did," laughed Chongo. "There ain't nothing wrong with your car."

She kept her eyes on the road and reached for a cigarette in her purse. "Yes . . . thanks."

He picked up the song he had been singing, something about "mi corazon," his arm stretched along the top of the seat.

"Would you like a cigarette?"

"Yeah. Thanks." He reached for the pack she held out and stopped. "Say, you got anything stronger than this? You don't have a joint, do you?"

She looked at him thoughtfully. "There's another pack of cigarettes in the glove compartment. Look in back."

He dumped out half the pack. Then came a skinny one.

"You're all right, honey," said Chongo as he lit up. "Ah, man, that tastes good. That's good stuff." He offered it to her, but she shook her head.

"No thanks, what I need now is an upper. I've got a long trip."

"Yeah, a long trip." He giggled and took a few more pulls. "Yeah, this stuff is, ah . . . like, wow."

She slowed down as he started nodding. By the time she pulled over, he was out. "I never did like Panama Red," she said to his crumpled form.

She opened the passenger door and lugged him out, into the ditch along the road. The posse would have no trouble finding him.

She turned the wagon around and sped back to the bridge. There was no one there. She parked on the other side of the road and got out, peering around her through the darkness. Then she raised the hood.

"Where you been?" he roared, shoving her back and slamming the hood down.

"Having my nails done, of course."

They got in and the tires rasped against the gravel as she accelerated. She told him about her other passenger.

He chuckled. "Chongo."

"Why did you let them go first?" she asked.

"Didn't want anyone climbing on my back." He turned toward her. "That reminds me. Was all this really necessary? Couldn't the U.S. of A. just pardon me?"

She looked at him as if he were something a dog had freshly eliminated, then turned back to the road. "You didn't think we were going to pardon a man who strangled his girlfriend, branded her with the letter 'A', and then left her hanging from a tree . . . did you?"

"It was an old oak tree," J.B. pointed out mournfully. "You have to get the symbolism." He stared out the side window and muttered, "She was a dumb cunt."

"I hear that's about all they found of her."

He was silent for a moment. Even now he could smell the scorched flesh as he stamped her rump with the branding iron, hammered into a lazy A. It was what had brought him out of his stupor after two days of drinking and alternately beating the corpse and caressing it. He had sunk his soul into that woman. Or something equally precious to his sense of manhood. And she had wrung it dry.

He flung his arm over the back of the seat. "I gave her two chances, you know. That was the third time she brought someone home and balled him—in my bed!"

He put his hand on the wheel. "Pull over."

She glanced at him. "We don't have time—."

"Now," he said quietly.

She parked off the road and turned toward him, her back pressed against the door. "Just what are you going to do with me, lady, when all this is over?"

"Why—we'll help you get started again—arrange for a new identity. You can go anywhere you want—."

Brown eyes a little scared now, he thought. Red hair straggling. That nice white flesh rising and falling under her sweater.

J.B. leaned back and stared straight ahead. "OK. Let's go."

* * *

They skirted Santa Fe, the city's lights strung out like a necklace across the plateau beneath the mountains, then turned south. The barest sliver of moon hung in the sky, and the road, narrow and sinuous, was black beyond the reach of the headlights. J.B. watched the dark humps of hills fall away, and then the land flattened out. He thought of asking where they were going, and then relaxed. What did it matter? He was out of the pen, and the unfettered air sang through his head. He closed his eyes. The rhythm of the road put him to sleep.

He woke once or twice as they slowed, going through a town. A handful of street lights, the bump of a railroad track, and the darkness sucked them in again.

Hours later, he heard a low rumble of voices, but he was too befogged to open his eyes. Then a long stretch of bumps irritated him. The road had disappeared and they were rocking over clumps of grass, rounding hills. A few miles more and the hills were gone, but not the jarring of his bones. He closed his eyes again, his feet set against the floorboard, and tried to merge with the motion of the wagon. When they stopped, the stillness came as a shock.

They had pulled up at a cluster of mobile homes.

"Here we are," she said, "home."

J.B. opened the door and hesitated. "By the way, what's your name?"

"You can call me Pandora."

He snorted. "OK, I'll keep my distance."

They seemed to be in the midst of a desert. Far to the east and west, it lapped up against menacing peaks.

"Where are we?" he demanded.

"White Sands Missile Range."

She led him to one of the trailers. It was fitted out with brown leather couches, lots of chrome and glass, and deep carpeting. The small refrigerator was stocked with food and a bucket of ice. He opened a cabinet above it. Sour mash and a couple of real glasses.

She was standing at the door. "See you tomorrow," she called, and disappeared before he could offer her a drink.

He poured the liquor into a glass and sipped slowly. Then he went outside and sat on the steps of the trailer. The wind was cold and he took deep breaths of it, staring up at a sky peppered with stars.

"Ah, Marybelle," he said aloud, "what have you brought me to? And where are you now?"

After a time he went inside and climbed into bed. He fell asleep with a vision of Marybelle balling the angel Gabriel.

Chapter 7

He squinted when he heard the knock on the door, and looked around for Chongo and Sammy and the others. Then he grinned. "Hold it!" he yelled, pulling on the terrycloth robe at the foot of the bed. He opened the door a crack and recoiled from the bright sun.

"We're having a breakfast meeting in the big trailer," Pandora said, from under a cowboy hat. "Ten minutes." She turned and strode off, levis undulating.

Hmmm. It was not going to be so easy, staying out of Pandora's box.

Inside, he found a wardrobe suited to a well-heeled tourist roughing it in the desert—blue jeans, western shirts, leather jackets, boots and hat. He pulled out a red plaid shirt. It was the farthest thing from prison gray he could find. Hunching so he could see his face in the bathroom mirror, he ran a hand over his cheeks, down to the scratchy jawline. Funny, he hadn't noticed those lines in his forehead before, or the one near a corner of his mouth. Oh, well, they hadn't spirited him away for his good looks.

Walking over to the largest of the half-dozen mobile homes, J.B. examined his surroundings. Tufts and tussocks of wild grasses erupted from the reddish earth, impeding his march, but in the distance they merged into a level expanse of green. An occasional hill, stubbled with piñon trees, like the chin of a man with a week-old growth of beard, broke the surface. To the north, spurs of black volcanic rock floated on the green. A range of mountains rose to the east and to the west, not menacing now, but pale and stolid. Nowhere on the plain could he see any vegetation taller than mesquite, or the shaft of a yucca. Yup, it was a desert, and as cut off from the rest of the world as any place you could want for a surreptitious and perhaps unrespectable undertaking.

There were four men seated around a large oak table in the big trailer, while Pandora poured coffee.

"Woman's work is never done," J.B. smiled, and slid past her onto a black leather couch. Her look of cold contempt followed him.

The large portly man named Arthur made the introductions, and they shook hands. Bob, short and slender, let his fingers graze J.B.'s. He flicked his eyes up and lowered them quickly. Carl had a sincere grip, the kind that inspired confidence, and Sam pumped his hand slowly, studying him from under thick black brows.

"Well, my boy," Arthur began. J.B. made a note never to trust the son-of-a-bitch. "I'm sure you're wondering why we went to all that trouble to bring you here."

"Yes, sir." Pandora glanced at him, but he continued to gaze at Arthur.

"You're no doubt aware of the grave situation facing our nation . . . our dependence on foreign oil, the price-gouging by the Arabs, the slowdown of production in Iran, and their humiliating actions."

J.B. waited.

"What we propose," Arthur continued, leaning toward J.B., "is to drill a pipeline all the way to Iran's oil fields . . . and suck the place dry." He leaned back smiling. There was silence. "Well," he leaned forward again, "that's why we need you. You can do it, can't you?"

J.B. shook his head. "I was afraid that's what you had in mind. Frankly, I don't know."

Arthur frowned. "Are you trying to hold us up, young man? We've already gotten you out of prison, in spite of that . . . heinous deed of yours." He pulled out a handkerchief and brushed at his lips.

"It's not that, Arthur. I suppose you're thinking of the laser drilling I've done. But it's never been tried on a big scale. And you're talking about going some five thousand miles." He shook his head again. "That's a lot of earth to slice through."

Carl folded his arms on the table. "We can get you anything you need, Craddock. You tell us what you want, it's yours."

"I want some assurances—that I won't be flushed down the tubes when this is over," J.B. replied.

"You've got them," Sam declared. "From the highest authority in the country."

"I want something in writing."

"What are you going to do with it," Sam laughed, "hide it in your shoe?"

"This thing might not work, you know," J.B. warned.

"Look, J.B.," Sam smiled, "we're not about to drive up to the pen with you and say, 'Sorry, we made a mistake, you can have him back.'" They stared at each other. "You give it your best shot, J.B., and then you're on your own."

J.B. gazed up at the ceiling. Who would he send an incriminating document to, anyway? His sister would tear it up without reading it. And who would believe such a wild-eyed story? He watched the sunlight bouncing off the light fixture overhead.

"Where do we get the laser?"

"From Los Alamos," said Carl. He moved around to J.B.'s side and began talking rapidly. J.B. watched the others slipping away.

"What? Sorry, I missed that."

Carl patiently reiterated that the brains and equipment of the scientific laboratory were practically at their beck and call.

"Now," he said, eyes shining, "let me show you around your laboratory."

J.B. followed him outside. Sunlight struck him from above, from below. He was not used to such bright light after being cooped up in the pen. Pandora had made one slip. At least, he assumed it was she who had selected his wardrobe. He'd have to get her to buy him a pair of sunglasses.

Carl had his arms spread and seemed to be waltzing.

"We're smack in the middle of the military reservation," he said, "about fifty miles from anywhere, including Trinity, the atomic bomb site. So when they do open the place to visitors, we'll still be out of the way."

"When do they open it?" J.B. asked.

"Changes every year. So the crazies can't organize a demonstration, I guess. But we'll get some notice."

Carl led him over to a blue trailer. Inside J.B. found a spacious workroom. One wall was lined with books, apparently every reference work a self-respecting geophysicist would have on hand. There was a long work table, a desk, maps and diagrams and models, and a calculator.

Carl waited until J.B. had looked over the room. Then he lifted the corner of a Navajo rug and flipped it over. He slipped his fingers into a crevice and pulled up a trap door and motioned to J.B. to follow him.

They climbed down steps into a chamber about twenty feet by forty feet. It was completely empty, waiting.

"We just made a steel box," said Carl, "and sank it into the ground. Figured this was as good a place as any to start drilling."

J.B. nodded. It was spooky down here, without any windows. He felt claustrophobic.

"I suppose you want to get started right away," he said.

Carl dropped the boyish bureaucrat tone. "You've been through a hell of a lot, J.B. Why don't you take the day off?"

★ ★ ★

It was almost noon when J.B. returned to his quarters. He popped the top on a can of beer and turned the television set on. He was out of prison, but they still had him boxed in. Fifty miles from nowhere, smack in the middle of nothing.

A shot of the penitentiary came on the screen and he sprang up to turn up the volume. ". . . state penitentiary last night, after cutting through the bars of a cell window, and cutting the double fence enclosing the facility. A foot patrol found the break in the fences approximately one hour after the inmates made their escape, and notified the warden."

The warden's face appeared, and then that of Chongo. "Martinez was found unconscious in a ditch along the highway fifteen miles from the prison, about two hours after the escape, apparently the victim of a drug overdose."

Poor Chongo, J.B. smiled. He's used to homegrown weed.

"State police found Rodriguez and Sloane early this morning, alerted by a homeowner who heard them scuffling outside her house."

Well, that was good news. He hoped Everett wouldn't be out too long, either. Bunch of creeps. He almost dropped the can of beer when his own face filled the screen. ". . . and J.B. Craddock, convicted of murder." J.B. sank back into the couch, as if to escape from that gray, glazed face under a spill of black hair.

". . . still have no idea how the men cut through the window bars or the two barbed-wire fences."

J.B. snapped the set off. He had taken the saw blade with him. Might come in handy again.

Chapter 8

Arthur left quietly the next day, in one of the four-wheel-drive wagons parked before the main trailer. Bob and Sam were officially on vacation, and would hang around for a while, at least until the project was organized and underway.

Bob was intoxicated with the scenery. He made short excursions out from the huddle of trailers, cameras and light meters hanging from his neck, a canteen buckled to his waist, a book on desert survival clutched in his hand . . . although he never ventured more than a mile away. He could be seen from time to time, slogging up a hill, framing a distant range of mountains with thumbs and forefingers, then snapping in every direction.

Once or twice he tried to coax Sam into going along, but the chief aide waved him off. "Too much fresh air," he growled, going back into his trailer. He spent most of his time watching television, occasionally jotting down notes and cackling about some particularly brilliant ploy he would use in the next electoral campaign.

Carl at first hovered at J.B.'s side, ready to be of help, until J.B. bumped him with his elbow a few times, and made it clear he preferred to work alone.

There was another matter. He felt guilty whenever he spaced out and then caught Carl watching him anxiously. It was hard for him to get back into the routine of work. He had spent his waking hours for three years obsessed with the problems of mere survival. Whether to fall into a clique or try to make it as a loner. Whether to work in the machine shop or in the laundry. Whether to carry a shank. Whom to watch out for in the showers. How to avoid being a snitch . . . or appearing to be one. Most of all, wondering why he had bothered to kill a dumb cunt like Marybelle, instead of just kicking her the hell out.

Now he had an honest-to-goodness job—well, relatively honest. And he found it difficult not to drift, to turn off the present and wander into a fantasy that spent the hours, as he had learned to do at the pen.

Then there was the work itself. It scared hell out of him. He had been away from the technology for so long, he wasn't sure he could do it, though he would never admit that to Arthur, or even Carl. He felt clumsy moving about in the workroom, and adding and subtracting figures seemed a chore. How would he ever plot a course to drill through the earth, and hit a target maybe a few miles wide and deep?

Well, all the materials were here, the books and measuring instruments. And he could order anything he needed. Thank God he was the only one who knew how inept he was. Concentration, that's what he needed. Concentrate, and take one step at a time. Hell, who else would even attempt to do the job he'd taken on? No one would be crazy enough to put his reputation on the line for such a scheme. Well, he had little enough reputation to worry about now . . . a convict on the loose. And there weren't all that many people who had been doing the laser work he'd been experimenting with a few years ago. Or who'd come up with that particular device for homing in on a reservoir of oil miles beneath the surface. Why not? If anyone could do it, it could just as easily be J.B. Craddock. But not with Carl panting over his shoulder.

The problems, however, were enormous, and not just in terms of miles. As soon as J.B. solved one, another, seemingly more insurmountable, cropped up.

First of all, they were going to have to drill through a hundred and fifty-six degrees of longitude, about four thousand, two hundred and seventy miles. Initially, J.B. calculated the path of the laser would slice through the outer core of the earth, miring them in molten rock. Totally unfeasible. He calculated again. Now he found they would slip through the inner edge of the mantle, avoiding the core.

The tiny orifice made by the laser would never accommodate the flow of oil, of course. They would need a shaft about eighteen inches in diameter. That would give them enough room for the equipment that would have to be put down the hole to extract the oil. And that meant they would have to vaporize thirty-nine million, eight hundred and forty-one thousand and three hundred and sixty cubic feet of rock. Flash Gordon, where are you, he moaned.

What kind of laser was going to vaporize that much rock in less than a millenium? He pictured himself with a beard down to his belly, patiently tending the instrument as its beam rotated somewhere deep underneath Mississippi.

Carbon dioxide. CO_2 lasers had been used before for deep drilling. They would need a continuous beam if they were ever going to get the job done. He envisioned the beam blasting doggedly through foot after foot after foot.... Uh, uh. No good. The stress would present too great a risk of cave-ins. They would do better delivering the energy in discrete pulses.

The ruby laser? J.B. pursed his lips in thought. The good old stand-by, first laser that had been constructed, and it still was the workhorse of the industry. The neodymium-yag was a respectable variation, with a high energy output. Maybe.

J.B. turned to the calculator. Tap, tap, tap. Sixty-nine thousand years? Oh, my God. He hid his face in his arms. Maybe he'd be better off hitchhiking up to Santa Fe and turning himself in. Only about twenty-seven more years in bondage to the state before he could apply for parole.

He raised his head and stretched it toward the pocked white ceiling of the trailer. There's got to be a better way.

Maybe if he jogged, got the blood moving through his limbs and long neglected brain. He pushed away from the desk and strode out the door. The sun immediately aimed a blazing ray at him, and he flinched. Solar energy, that's what we need. How about a nice controlled hydrogen explosion? He took a few tentative steps. Where was the starting line? Oh, hell. Feeling like a fool, he broke into a run. Yeah. Yeah!

The ever present wind sluiced past his ears, lapped his neck. Ahead of him stretched grass and blue sky and more grass. Two hundred yards out he slowed to a walk. He panted up a hill and stopped at the crest, waiting for his breathing to slow. Turning, he surveyed the trailers in the distance, looking like the remnants of some giant's kitchen midden, here in this sun-blighted waste. He grimaced. Staring at his feet, he plodded back to camp. He stopped at his trailer to pick up a cold beer before returning to the lab.

An almost imperceptible movement registered at the periphery of his vision. Was it a trick of light, a reaction to his mad dash into the desert? Or was Pandora, ever alert, watching from her window? He tipped the can up in the direction of her trailer and took a swallow. Take that, cop.

Hunched over the calculator again, J.B. punched in numbers until his fingers ached. By the end of the day, there was a scowl etched into his face.

Chapter 9

By the end of the first week, he had the time down to a mere one hundred and ninety-three years. By means of Q-switching, attaching a rotating prism to the emitting end of the laser, he could build up the intensity of the beam and increase the lasing power tremendously. Add a few mirrors here, a few lenses there, all easily controlled by a computer, and the power increased still more. But not enough.

There had to be something else. J.B. reread all the literature on the neodymium-yag rod. He checked and rechecked his figures. Nothing moved.

He moped around for the next few days, completely absorbed in his problem, isolated from any world beyond that of the neodymium-yag laser. Sleepwalking from trailer to workroom to the big trailer for meals, and often skipping them, he hardly spoke to anyone, and grunted when spoken to.

Once a week, a van from the White Sands commissary appeared, unloading food and drink at the Washington Club West, as Sam had named the big trailer. He and the others were free to cook for themselves in their own quarters, but generally they gravitated to the club in the evenings for communal dinners. Pandora had tacitly been designated chief cook, although Bob took an occasional turn, and she served up elegant meals with more or less good will, moving efficiently in levis or a pantsuit. J.B. was too tired to be very interested.

One night he dreamed he was being impaled by a huge rod of ruby. Another night, he found himself wandering through a forest of translucent trees, whose sap he could see rising and falling. When he emerged, he looked back to see that the trees were laser rods, pulsing with electrons.

He saw laser rods all around him—in the water pipes beneath the kitchen sink, in the cardboard mailing tubes in which Sam received some magazines, in the sausage links on his breakfast plate.

"J.B., are you all right?"

"What?" J.B. looked up one night to find Pandora staring at him across the dinner table.

"I said, are you all right? We were talking, and you seemed to fade out."

"Of course I'm all right," he retorted, clutching a can of beer. He raised it to his lips. Empty. Disgustedly, he began to crumple it with both hands. Light bounced off the planes of flattened aluminum. He regarded them vaguely, then turned the can slowly.

"What is it?" Sam asked.

"Nothing," he replied, a little too quickly. He saw the worried looks on their faces and leaned back in his chair. "Nothing," he murmured.

* * *

Why does a rod have to be a rod, he repeated to himself in the lab the next day. He pulled books off a shelf and flipped through them. What was that angle again? "Brewster, Brewster," he said aloud, running his finger down an index. Ah. He flipped back. Fifty-seven degrees . . . .

He drew a clean yellow legal pad toward him, stuck the end of a pen in his mouth and hesitated. Then he began drawing.

Twenty minutes and several sketches later, he sat back to admire his artwork. He took a deep breath and expelled it loudly through his mouth. Let's see what those bozos up in Los Alamos can do with that, he grinned.

* * *

Arthur reappeared suddenly. At dinner, he poked suspiciously at yogurt-topped crepes, then pushed his plate away. "Well?" he asked, directing his gaze at J.B.

"Sir?"

"Where do we stand? What have you accomplished, young man?"

J.B. took a sip of wine and broke off a chunk of broccoli with his fork. "I'll have something for you tomorrow." He munched and swallowed. "If that's all right."

Arthur looked down at his plate, hesitated, and pulled it toward him.

Afterwards, he leaned back contentedly. "That was delicious, Pandora," he intoned, "very . . . interesting."

"Good, I'm glad you liked it, Arthur," smiled Pandora. She had carried her plate to the kitchen and returned wiping her hands on a dish towel. She tossed the towel over his paunch and leaned forward, fists on hips. "Because tomorrow it's your turn!"

Arthur glared at her for five seconds before capitulating. "I'll get you a cook tomorrow."

Chapter 10

J.B. had invited them all to the lab the next morning. They crowded at the long table, examining the model J.B. had constructed. All except Carl, who half sat on the end, arms folded complacently.

J.B. pulled up the only two chairs in the room and slowly inserted himself between the group and the table. Arthur and Sam sat down, and Bob and Pandora retreated against the library wall.

"As you can see," J.B. began, pulling the big lopsided ball toward him, "this is the earth. Over here," he raised one finger, "is White Sands. Here," he raised the finger of the other hand, "we have Iran." He lifted off the top fourth of the three-foot-diameter model and leaned the bottom section toward them. It was covered with a sheet of cardboard painted in concentric circles of varying widths.

"What we have to do," he continued, "is drill a straight path from here . . . to here. That's well below the surface of the oil field, but should put us in the ballpark, according to the information we've assembled." He glanced at Carl, who nodded, then returned to the model. "We'll be going through the mantle." He pointed to one of the circles. "That means about forty-two hundred miles of rock."

Arthur frowned. "Do you mean we have to put in a pipeline four-thousand miles long?"

"No," J.B. shook his head. "The lasing action will fuse the surrounding rock as we go, creating a nice little tunnel, about eighteen inches in diameter."

"But," Arthur argued, "how do we get the oil out?"

"Gravity, partly. The oil will flow down toward the earth's core." He pointed to where the middle of the laser's course would be. "We get fairly close to the outer core about here. The pressure of the oil will push it a little farther along. Then, from about here on . . . maybe two thousand miles . . . we'll have to pump up." He stopped and looked at Arthur.

The defense secretary grunted. "How long will it take to drill the tunnel?"

J.B. sighed and looked up at the ceiling. "Well, my first estimate was about sixty-nine thousand years." He looked down as Arthur's jaw dropped. "Then I added a few twists, made some more calculations, and came up with one hundred ninety-three years." Arthur's eyes seemed to be receding, and J.B. took his time.

"Well, I assumed you'd want to accomplish the job in one man's lifetime, so through a process of reasoning and omphaloskepsis, I—."

"Who?" Arthur hooted.

Sam chuckled. "That means he studied his navel." Arthur sank his head into one hand.

"Anyway, I came up with a new design for the laser," J.B. continued, pulling out his sketch. "Instead of a rod, it's a six-sided prism. It's angled so that we get total internal reflection—the pumping light from our flashlamp, which powers the laser, just keeps bouncing around inside, building up the intensity of the lasing action, so we get a significant increase in output."

"And?" Arthur prompted.

"I think we can get the power to do it in five years. If everything goes perfectly, without a hitch, we might do it in two."

Arthur leaned back and the others relaxed. "That's more like it," the secretary said.

J.B. waited until the group had settled down before he went on quietly. "I have to emphasize that everything will have to work perfectly, and we'll have to be damned lucky, because the drilling is the easy part."

"What do you mean?" Sam asked.

Now J.B. frowned as he moved from the glamour to the grit. "After a few thousand feet, we're going to have to lower the laser down into the shaft, because the beam diverges with distance, although it spreads out very slowly, and then it won't vaporize anything. This in itself is a problem. I'll have to rig something to keep the laser steady. Assuming we solve that problem, sooner or later we're bound to run into a bigger one before we get to Iran—some kind of pressurized zone that could blow the laser all to hell. It could be a pocket of gas, or oil, or an explosive magma chamber.

"If we're lucky, that laser spectrometer I developed will tell us in time, and we can pull the laser up. We'll take frequent readings, so we'll know what we're getting into. If it's a pocket of oil or gas, we can set up a conventional drilling operation, lay some pipe down until we're through the pocket, and then go on with the laser. But as you can imagine, all this will take time."

Arthur nodded morosely.

"But if we do strike oil," J.B. brightened, "maybe you'll want to stop right there, Arthur."

The secretary's eyes narrowed. "The object of this exercise," he pointed out, "is twofold: to acquire a reserve of oil, and to deprive Iran of it."

"So we go on?"

"We go on."

J.B. nodded. "Well, we'll give it our best shot." He suddenly realized the attraction of the editorial "we."

Sam brushed cigar ashes off his pants. "Tell us about the laser, J.B.," he said.

J.B. folded his arms. "Except for the design modification, it's just your standard neodymium-yag laser. The whole assembly is about eight feet long. Should take us about two or three weeks to have it fabricated and get everything set up."

"What's a yag?" Bob asked.

"Yttrium aluminum garnet. It's a variation of the original ruby laser. Neodymium ions are imbedded in it."

Now Pandora chimed in. "J.B., how can you be sure this thing is going to wind up in Iran . . . instead of Istanbul, or Kalamazoo?"

J.B. rubbed his chin. "Well, of course, we'll be checking the direction of the shaft as we go. But assuming I've plotted the course correctly, and the oil pool extends to where we think it does, the laser beam will go straight to our target. A laser emits a beam that's, well, straight as an arrow."

"Hey," Bob exclaimed, "that's great! Let's call the project 'Straight Arrow.'"

"Yah," said Sam, "just the thing to give the Ayatollah the shaft."

Above the laughter, Sam asked, "But how do we know when we've arrived?"

"Good question. The spectrometer should tell us. And we'll have a pretty good idea of how fast we're moving after a few days."

He began tidying the papers on the table as Arthur rose and the others prepared to follow. Then he turned back to Arthur. "Oh, one thing more."

Arthur looked pained.

"We'll be running the laser twenty-four hours a day, if we expect to get there in our lifetime. We'll need a couple more people to monitor the operation."

"You'll have them," Arthur declared, striding quickly out the door.

Chapter 11

J.B. looked up once the next day, as a jeep rocked over the ground and came to a stop at the Washington Club West. After exchanging a corporal, apparently the new cook, for Arthur, who was off to Washington East again, the jeep disappeared.

J.B. turned back to Carl, and resumed his explanations of his sketches and diagrams.

Sometime in midafternoon, Carl pushed his stack of notes aside and leaned back. "Looks like a winner, J.B.," he said.

"We'll only know when we fire it up."

Carl nodded. "I'd better leave for Los Alamos this afternoon and get things underway. You get some rest," he advised, rising. "After all, the worst is yet to come." He laughed and J.B. forced a chuckle.

"Yeah, maybe I'll take in the sights."

Carl thumped him on the back as he left, and J.B. turned to slump in a chair. Carl, old buddy, you don't know how right you are, he thought. Because I've only solved the first half of the puzzle. And I'm not even sure of that.

The question is, how do I put that laser down in the hole and keep it pointing toward Iran?

* * *

By evening, J.B. had managed to push the problem to the back of his mind. He was looking forward to seeing a new face, after the last few claustrophobic weeks with the Washington crowd. He whistled as he sauntered toward the main trailer, wondering whether army food had changed since his stint in Korea thirty years before.

He conjured up a skinny kid from West Virginia. No, probably a wisecracking Italian from New York.

He was not prepared for the round dark face that leaned out from behind the refrigerator door at his entrance. Under a wedge of black hair, black eyes flicked over him, and for an instant J.B. feared he had been recognized. Then the lips split in a blazing grin beneath the long mustaches, and the stocky body of the man appeared.

"Hi, I'm Alfredo Gutierrez," he said, his tongue caressing each vowel and syllable before letting it roll into the ether. There ought to be a "don" in front of it, thought J.B., or at least "general."

"But you can call me 'Alfie,'" he continued, thrusting out his hand.

"Mucho gusto," mumbled J.B., shaking hands. "You can call me 'J.B.'"

Alfie laughed and turned back to the stove. "Dinner's almost ready," he called over his shoulder. "You want a beer, man?"

"Sure." Alfie quickly uncapped a Dos Equis and placed it before him. J.B. regarded the vapor rising from the icy bottle and smiled. The character of their encampment in the desert seemed to have changed, from an outcrop of sober bureaucrats bearing the fate of the Western, and Anglo, world, to a ranchería in Old Mexico. He looked around for a mariachi as Bob and Pandora entered. Sam straggled in after them.

The men had obviously met earlier. Alfie examined Pandora appreciatively as she introduced herself. "Pleased to meet you, ma'am," he said.

"What's for dinner?" Sam bawled. "I'm starved."

Alfie brightened. "Enchiladas, with green chile." He passed out beers. Pandora declined.

"I had chile once," Bob recalled, "at a Texas barbecue."

"Aah," Alfie sneered, waving away the vision. "They don't know how to make chile in Texas. They put in beans—beans!" he repeated indignantly, setting their plates on the table. "That stuff's just for tourists."

"I don't know," Bob protested weakly. "Seemed pretty good to me."

Alfie shook his head. "And their chile, man, it tastes like tomato sauce. It's got no bite, man," he marvelled.

Bob and Pandora exchanged dubious looks.

"Where'd you get this chile?" J.B. asked casually, forking it around his plate.

"Hatch," Alfie replied. "Just across the mountains from here. They really know how to grow chile, man." J.B. smiled. He had eaten Hatch chile in the pen.

Sam dug into his plate and chomped with relish. "Great!" he pronounced, taking a swig of beer.

Heartened by his enthusiasm, Bob and Pandora began to take tentative bites. J.B. pierced the egg on top and let it run into the green sauce. He picked up a forkful along with some rice. It was good, he agreed silently, full of flavor and—.

Pandora gasped. "Water," she whispered. "Water." Alfie brought her a glass as she began coughing.

Hot as hell, J.B. finished his thought. "Here," he said, pushing his beer toward her. She waved it away, taking a sip of water. But the coughing continued. J.B. held the beer up to her, insisting. Desperate, she took a swallow. Then she sat back panting while Alfie giggled and Sam chortled.

"Thanks," she muttered, glaring at Sam.

"It's the only thing that'll put out the fire," J.B. remarked, taking another bite along with refried beans, and following it with a chunk of tortilla. Pandora drew a deep breath before following his example.

Bob was making a great show of eating, but J.B. noticed he was concentrating on the beans and rice at the side of the plate, picking only occasionally at the chile. Finally he gave up. Sam's empty plate stared at him like a reproof.

"You must have a cast-iron stomach," he moaned.

"Not at all," said Sam mildly. "It's just that real men like Hatch chile."

He glanced toward the kitchen. "Alfie, I'll take another tortilla."

"Coming up, boss," Alfie responded, "but leave some room for dessert."

The rich custard went down more smoothly. Alfie, arms folded, watched them as they finished.

"Maybe I'll make the red chile tomorrow," he mused. "It's usually not so hot."

Pandora closed her eyes. "What else do you have in your repertoire?"

Alfie pulled at his mustache. "How about beef stroganoff? Chicken cacciatore? I don't dig this Nouvelle Cuisine too much, that the generals' wives are always asking for. You need something that sticks to the ribs."

For the first time, Pandora laughed. "This will stick with me all night, Alfie," she assured him. "But that beef stroganoff sounds marvelous."

Sam pouted. "Can't you throw in a little chile once in a while?"

"Sure, boss. But I think I'll order some of the Chimayo stuff." He smiled at Pandora. "Don't want to lose a paying customer."

Chapter 12

J.B. put his boots up on the worktable and rocked back in the chair, clasping his hands behind his head. I'm going to sit here, he said to himself, until I get an answer.

It was too quiet in the workroom. He started whistling. That reminded him of Texas and Marybelle. He put his elbows on the table and studied the model of the earth. He imagined a stream of crude oozing from Iran, around the circumference.

Would the laser work, he wondered. By God, they were going to have to average five miles a day, if they were going to reach Iran in two years, or even five, given the delays he felt sure would be unavoidable. That brought him back to the problem of lowering the laser into the shaft.

Maybe a Dos Equis would inspire him.

He wandered over to the big trailer where Alfie was clanging pots, sniffing and tasting.

"Smells fantastic. What is that, chile stew?"

"No," Alfie replied wistfully, "just an ordinary little ragout."

"I've a feeling that nothing you do is ordinary," said J.B.

Alfie chuckled. "Well, I do have some nice shallots in it, and fresh cilantro," he admitted.

J.B. was mystified. "Where'd you learn to cook like that, Alfie?"

"Oh, the army sent me to gourmet school. You know, join the army, learn a trade?" He lifted a lid, dipped in a ladle, and noisily sipped. Licking his lips, he bobbed his head and replaced the lid.

"You from around here?" J.B. asked.

"No. Gary, Indiana."

"What!"

"Yeah," Alfie assured him. "They got a big Mexican, uh, Hispanic community there."

J.B. shook his head. "Gary, Indiana," he repeated. The world was changing. Where had he been? But, of course, he knew precisely where he had been.

"Must be pretty boring for you out here, tending a bunch of—civilians, out in the middle of nowhere."

"Hey, no, man," Alfie protested, sitting down opposite J.B., with his arms folded on the table. "This place is great. I mean, it gives me time for my project."

"Your project?"

"Yeah," Alfie said. "I got this idea I been working on for years, man. It's gonna solve the energy crisis."

J.B.'s head snapped up and he stared sharply at Alfie. "What project is that?" he asked, eyes narrowed.

Alfie glanced conspiratorially around the empty trailer and leaned forward. "I don't like to tell many people about it, you know, because they don't understand."

J.B. nodded sympathetically. "I understand."

"It's this box I'm developing," Alfie almost whispered. "You see," he said, scouring the room again, "it captures the energy from Alpha Centauri. That's the closest star to the earth, you know."

"Yes. I know." J.B. felt his mind go into a coasting mode. He watched Alfie's lips form and unform words. The sounds eluded him. Isn't anybody sane out here, he wondered. He nodded as Alfie continued miming words, and slipped farther and farther into his own head. The late afternoon sun sent a shaft of light penetrating the dust-laden space between them. The sun, source of all earthly energy. He wondered what Copernicus' wife would have said—if he had had a wife—when the old man came home one day and announced he'd discovered that the earth revolved around the sun. "How amazing! What a remarkable thing!" All the while thinking, "Oy, my poor Nicky, he's his own Polish joke."

The world was full of applications of ideas that had amused sophisticated salons a hundred, even fifty, years ago, he reflected. He himself was about to use a beam of light to bore through steel and rock. Well, maybe.

And what was so outlandish about it, after all? Just a few miles down the road, they were rehearsing the end of the world, shooting into the stratosphere practice missiles that one day would be tipped with nuclear warheads. Now, *that* was outlandish.

"That's really an amazing—. What a remarkable—," he heard himself saying, as Alfie seemed to draw himself to attention. He turned around to see Sam's cherubic face and grinned.

"Right away, boss, lunch is almost ready," Alfie chattered.

Chapter 13

"Ten days at most. Maybe a week," Carl exulted upon his return, "and they'll have the laser, and then we could be embarking upon the most historic project in the annals of humankind."

J.B. nodded. It was appalling how the promise of an unlimited source of energy could turn the minds of rational men into sour mash. There must be as many ideas for solving the energy crisis as there were schemes for escaping from the state pen. Maybe it was the modern version of searching for the Fountain of Youth.

And here he was, nodding again to the rhythm of someone else's fantasy.

* * *

He was back at the desk the next morning. He wrote out the question on a slip of paper, as if seeing it might stimulate an answer: How to put the laser down the hole?

Attach a gyroscope to keep it on course? No. He'd need some kind of track the laser could ride on. Maybe encase everything in pipe. But how could they add pipe, with those miles of cables hanging out, like some gigantic placenta? There was the power cable, the computer cable, the air hose, the water hoses . . . .

J.B. saw himself splicing the power cable, then—. Oh, my God. How are you going to splice the water hoses, you dummy? Not to mention all the water tanks that would be needed.

His feet dropped to the floor and he was up on them the next instant, pacing the room, one fist pounding his thick skull. Maybe he should have gone with the CO_2 laser. The flowing gas cooled itself.

How would he cool the neodymium-yag laser without a stream of water? Pack it in dry ice. Yeah, that would last about five minutes.

He sat down at the desk and doodled with a pen, letting his thoughts go free. Dry ice. Refrigeration. Just pack the whole thing into a refrigerator. No. Maybe the other way around.

Let's start from scratch, he thought. Imagine a self-contained unit—well, almost self-contained—with its own cooling system. What kind? He went to the wall of books and scanned the titles impatiently, running his finger over the spines. Finally it stopped at a volume on coolants. At the desk he pored over a few pages, skipped to another section and pored over that. Well, he wasn't about to become an expert, but he began to visualize a mini-refrigeration system that would fit within the laser housing. Liquid nitrogen might be appropriate. Maybe the excess heat could be drawn off through the air hose, along with the vaporized rock.

He drew several diagrams, made a few notations and stopped. "Hell," he breathed, that ought to be enough to get the boys at Los Alamos started. Let them work out the details. But he'd better talk to Carl immediately and have him stop the work on his original design.

"Self-contained unit" replayed in his head as he hurried out. By the time he reached Carl's trailer, he thought he had the answer to his other problem.

There was no answer to his knock.

"Carl!" he yelled, pounding on the door. The wind came up and whirred past his ear. What now, he thought.

He turned and headed for Sam's place. Again no answer. He felt abandoned. Where had everyone gone?

Pandora was washing her hair when he knocked at her trailer.

"Where's Carl?" he asked. "I need him."

"He went back to Washington, with Sam."

"Don't tell me they trust me alone out here with you?" J.B. smirked.

"Bob's still here." She pulled the bathrobe closer around her shoulders. "If there's anything you need, maybe I—."

"No, I have to talk to Carl." He stuffed his hands in his pockets and squinted up at the sky. "Well, it's about the laser. We've got to stop the work at Los Alamos. I changed the design."

"I think I can get a message to him," Pandora said sarcastically.

"When will he be back?"

"I don't know. There's some problem about the money."

Chapter 14

"He what?" howled Sam.

"He nominated it for 'Boondoggle of the Month,' biggest waste of the taxpayers' money," said the president.

"*Mister* President," Sam said icily. "Do you mean that this project—which could mean life or death for the Western world—is being imperiled by a lousy senator?"

The secretary of energy leaned his head against his hand. "You don't have to write speeches for us, Sam."

"Why are you so incensed?" asked the president. "I thought you were skeptical of the whole idea."

"I changed my mind," Sam muttered. "The last time I filled up my gas tank."

"Whose idea was this anyhow," Arthur asked, "putting it in the budget of the National Academy of Sciences?"

"Mine!" The secretary of energy was defensive. "I thought it was a natural—Project Dowser: A proposal to test the feasibility of locating petroleum through psychotronic devices."

"Naturally," Sam sneered. "Don't you know that guy loves to go through the academy's budget with a fine-toothed comb?"

"Personally," sniffed the president, "I've always admired the man for pointing out capricious uses of the taxpayers' money."

Arthur massaged his paunch and shook his head. "You should have put it in my budget. No one would have the audacity to question a measly five-million-dollar item for defense."

"So what do we do now?" Sam asked.

"I suppose we can have the grant withdrawn," Carl suggested, looking at his boss.

"And I'll add a little item in the defense budget for administrative expenses," Arthur smiled.

"Will that shut him up?" Sam asked.

The president studied his fingernails. "I'll have Gloria invite him to dinner with the Russian ballet corps. He has a soft spot for that skinny blonde from Omsk."

Chapter 15

J.B.'s anxiety grew as the time for the arrival of the laser neared. To pass the time and dull his doubts, he let himself be cajoled into a poker game with Sam, Bob and Alfie.

"Sorry, gents," he announced as he took his seat, "I'll have to play with matchsticks. My keeper hasn't given me an allowance."

"What!" exclaimed Bob. Alfie looked puzzled. Sam slid over a fifty.

J.B. cleared his throat. It appeared this was going to be a serious game.

Three hands and twenty-five dollars later, J.B. realized why Bob had been so outraged at his declaration. The man was a master of the game. His boyish enthusiasm had disappeared and his face was a mask of studied indifference. The pile of money in front of him was growing.

Oh, well, it wasn't as if it were his money. J.B. finessed a pair of jacks into a winner, and raked in a pot. It was the highlight of his day.

Half an hour later he was an observer, broke again, watching the faces and styles of the three men.

Alfie had a habit of twisting his mustache whenever he had something promising. He tugged at his ear when he didn't.

Sam looked perpetually angry, glaring at his cards. Occasionally he took the time to flick his cigar at an ashtray, signaling that he was on to something.

Bob's eyes moved rhythmically from hand to pot to each player's face in turn, detecting every twitch and grimace.

Carl joined them, watching over J.B.'s shoulder.

"Grab a chair and some money," Sam suggested.

Carl declined the invitation. "I know when I'm out of my league."

"Where you been all day?" Sam asked, seemingly grateful for an interruption in Bob's onslaught.

"I've got some reports to write up for the secretary. I'll have to get back to it after dinner."

Sam had forgotten the question. He chomped on the cigar as he watched Bob gather in another pot.

"That cleans me out," he growled. He looked up at Alfie.

"Yeah," Alfie agreed sadly. "I better get to work, anyhow."

"Great game," Bob smiled, as he finished counting his loot. "That's enough to get me a new wide-angle lens for the camera."

Sam scowled at the stump of his cigar. "Glad to help."

Chapter 16

"Alfie," Bob moaned, "what's taking so long? Where are my eggs?"

"Coming right up," Alfie replied from the kitchen, "and so is a big truck. You guys expecting a package?"

Bob and J.B. bolted for the window. A large van, unmarked and painted a nauseating olive-drab, was slowly advancing. J.B. felt his stomach sink. He watched reality growing larger, beating its way relentlessly through the squirming heat waves, like a juggernaut.

A young black man with a manicured beard swung down from the passenger seat.

"We've got a delivery here for Carl Saunders." J.B. hesitated at the unfamiliar last name before stepping forward.

"Carl's not here today," he said. "I'll show you where it goes."

He pointed out the laboratory. "That's it over there."

"Great. Why don't you hop in?"

J.B. hoisted himself up and nodded at the other two men in the truck. He glanced at the crates in back and sat down. The truck lurched forward, then rolled smoothly the two hundred feet to the trailer.

J.B. opened the door. Behind him, two of the men opened the rear doors of the van and let down a ramp. Gingerly they slid the largest of the crates down to the ground. Then they hoisted it and followed him into the workroom and down the stairs to the empty chamber. The workmen broke down the crate quickly. The white fiberglass housing of the laser gleamed. Now J.B. directed them as they maneuvered it into place, within a cradle he had constructed and lined up with the guidelines he had chalked on the floor.

The young man stared at the business end of the laser, pointing down toward the floor.

"Well," he drawled, "I guess you're planning to drill a hole to China."

J.B. joined in the laughter. "Maybe not quite that far," he smiled.

"We've got your generator, too," said the young man, starting back up the stairs, "and the air pump . . . and the coaxial and other cables. At least, the first shipment. We'll be bringing in more."

"And the computer?"

"The computer, too."

"I hope you're going to set it up for me," J.B. said anxiously. "That's not my strong suit."

"Sure thing," said the man.

Within an hour, the men had arranged all the equipment and attached the various cables.

The system looked like an oversized recumbent vacuum cleaner, with the air tube projecting a few feet from the front of the housing. Snaking out in back were the coaxial cable, the air hose and the cable leading to the computer. The spectrometer sat on top of the housing like a wary eye. The whole assembly, eight feet in length, rode on four small wheels.

"Well, might as well get started," the young man said, sitting down at the computer console. "By the way, I'm Jake Hagstrom."

"Jim," was J.B.'s curt reply, as he extended his hand. Jake registered the abbreviated name before turning back to the console. He was accustomed to receiving only as much information as was necessary to his work.

Now, as J.B. explained how the laser was to work, Jake programmed the computer to control the mirrors and lens inside, and to process information from the spectrometer. J.B. watched the operation avidly. With each flash of the lamp, the laser beam would produce a tiny hole about five millimeters in diameter. As the mirrors swiveled, one horizontally and one vertically, the beam would move, sweeping back and forth across the face of the rock, cutting out an elliptical shaft eighteen inches in diameter. The lens would keep the beam concentrated.

The shaft, however, would not be a perfect ellipse. The beam would leave a ridge a few inches high and about fourteen inches wide at the bottom of the shaft, creating a track at each side, over which the wheels of the assembly would move.

Jake leaned back and rubbed his eyes. "I think she's ready to go. Let's take a break and then I'll check her out."

They strolled back to the Washington Club West for lunch. Alfie was delighted with the company, but soon grew bored with the conversation, mostly a monologue by Jake on the merits of different personal computers. His two companions from Los Alamos ate silently.

After lunch, Jake gave the computer a trial run. He made a small adjustment before pronouncing all systems "go."

"OK," he said, "your turn."

J.B. was disconcerted. He had always been leery of computers and wasn't much more comfortable with one now.

"You've got to start sometime," Jake advised, "unless someone else is going to handle it for you."

J.B. shook his head and sat down at the console. Prompted by Jake, he began feeding instructions into the computer. From time to time he made notes.

A few hours and several Dos Equis later, he had a smile on his face. Not exactly a pro, but he felt confident he could manage the computer.

"When do you start?" Jake asked as he prepared to leave. And J.B. realized the moment was here. While they had been running the computer through its program, the other two men had been putting in the filtration system, boring a tunnel from the underground chamber to the outside for the air hose that would carry vapor sucked up from the target area to the surface. Another tunnel would permit the miles of cables to be wound up outside, when the laser was pulled up. Now everything was in place. There was no reason for delay.

"Tomorrow . . . I guess," he responded quietly.

"Well," Jake said, starting up the stairs, "see you in China."

* * *

He was still sitting there, studying his fiberglass monster, when Carl pattered down the stairs. The unconquerable optimism the man exuded roused him and he grinned.

"Lots of traffic out here today," Carl observed. "Was that the Los Alamos crew we passed on the way in?" His eyes swung to the laser.

"The same. How do you like their handiwork?"

Carl slid his hand lightly over the housing. "If you like it, I like it. But—it certainly looks like nothing I've ever seen before."

"How about something your wife cleans the house with?"

Carl laughed. "I'd sure like to see that prism of yours."

"Well, maybe I'll open it up . . . in about a month. We'll have to bring it up every once in a while to polish it, and to replace the flash lamp, of course."

Carl took in the equipment scattered around the chamber. "You ready to start?"

"I'll test it tomorrow." J.B. snapped his fingers. "That reminds me. Arthur promised to get two more men, so we can operate twenty-four hours a day."

"I'll mention it to him," Carl said. "He came back from Washington with me."

Chapter 17

Long before sunrise, J.B. was up drinking coffee. He watched the pearly glow creep up over the mountains, blush, then disintegrate into torn ribbons of orange and red.

He slipped on a jacket and opened the door carefully, trying not to make a sound. Somewhere a bird started up its morning song, sweetly trilling across the desert. J.B. felt like an ox crunching over the tufts of grass.

Down in the laboratory, he checked the angle of the laser, adjusted the cradle and checked it again, until it conformed precisely to the angle he had calculated with the help of a plumb line. Then he stared at the computer keyboard. Slow, go slow. He breathed deeply, clearing his mind of everything but the sequence of steps he would take.

He crossed the room and flicked the generator switch. A mild hum washed across the room. At the keyboard again, he flipped a lever and typed in "StArrow." A checkerboard of choices appeared, and he selected "lase." The clicks of the flash lamp were barely perceptible. He glanced at his watch. It was six fifty-one.

It was a few seconds before he realized a tiny cloud of vapor was forming on the floor in front of the beam opening. The laser itself made no sound, and of course the beam, being in the infrared sector of the spectrum, was invisible.

The cloud of vapor remained small. The air pump, at least, was working. But nothing seemed to be happening.

Six fifty-two. J.B. instructed the computer to stop lasing and hurried to the laser. The vapor was gone. Where it had been was the beginning of a shaft, with a neat, low ridge on the bottom.

Well, it works, J.B. breathed. But how much power was he getting? How deep was the tunnel?

Damn! He needed a tape measure. He ran up the steps and stood looking around him. He knew he'd seen one some place. Damn. Why wasn't he prepared for this? He scoured the desk. Maybe in a drawer. In the second one he tried, he found it.

He hurried back down. Maneuvering around the front end of the laser, he let the tape out slowly. Five feet . . . ten . . . fifteen . . . . The tape stuck at about twenty-one feet.

He sat down at the keyboard and grabbed pen and paper. If it does twenty-one feet in one minute . . . that's twelve hundred and sixty feet in an hour, and . . . thirty thousand, two hundred forty feet in a day. "Oh, my God," he whispered. "Five point seven miles in a day." They could do it in two years.

Of course, this was only the initial output, J.B. reflected. As the distance between the target area and the laser increased, the beam would diverge and its intensity diminish. The lens and the redesign of the rod would help correct that. But after several thousand feet, the beam would vaporize nothing. By that time, of course, he'd have the laser down in the hole. If he could keep it moving not more than a thousand feet from the rock face, the beam would maintain most of its intensity. Five point seven miles was ideal, but hell, he'd be happy with five miles a day.

What about the rock? J.B. punched a command into the computer. A pattern appeared on the screen, a fingerprint of the material being vaporized, transmitted by the spectrometer. It was the frequency for calcium carbonate. Likely enough.

Elated, J.B. turned off the equipment. Time for breakfast. He had earned it.

* * *

Sonny Rasmussen and Morgan Curtis arrived early that afternoon, along with the two trailers that would be their quarters. Arthur introduced them as engineers from the missile base who, with J.B., would take turns operating Straight Arrow.

Sonny was a big blond in his late twenties, enthusiastic and voluble. He had been a linebacker at Cal Tech, and had decided to join the army after a busted knee dashed his hopes of a pro football career.

Morgan, about thirty-five, was tall, slim and dark. Arthur mumbled something about MIT and he nodded, examining J.B. with expressionless hazel eyes. Another good poker player, J.B. thought.

He took them over to the lab and showed them around the equipment, explaining its functions and describing the problems that might arise.

"The most important thing is to monitor the cooling system." He showed them how to take a reading from the thermocouples in the air hose and the lasing head. "The temperature at the lasing head should be around five hundred and fifty degrees Fahrenheit," he explained. "A few degrees more or less won't hurt, but if it goes up significantly, shut everything down and call me immediately."

They nodded.

"The second most important thing is the spectrometer. Eventually we'll want to take a reading every five minutes or so. Right now, every fifteen minutes will do."

J.B. showed them drawings of several frequency patterns. "The computer will analyze the graphs, but I want you to see some samples. Now these are graphs of the different kinds of rock we're expecting to go through—nickel and iron mostly. Each spike corresponds to a particular element that's florescing."

He looked up at their blank faces. "Well, let's just say an element in the rock that's being vaporized by the lasing action." They nodded.

He picked up another sheaf of papers. "These are the ones we don't want to see—hydrocarbons, magma. If we see much benzene, it could be an indication we're close to a reservoir of oil. If there's any hint of any of these on the graph, shut down the works and call me. We'll lose the laser if we plow into a pool of oil or gas."

"Right," said Sonny. Morgan seemed to be committing the patterns to memory.

J.B. returned the papers to the computer desk. "I'll take the first shift, starting at eight. You two can decide who comes on next. It's going to get kind of boring, so we might change shifts every couple of weeks. Or even cut down to shifts of four hours."

"No problem," Morgan put in.

J.B. looked at his watch. "Two-thirty," he noted. "Well, we might as well start right now." He walked over to the generator and turned it on. "I'm going to run it for an hour and three-quarters and lase down to about two thousand feet. Then first thing tomorrow, you can help me put the laser down into the shaft."

He swung around in the chair and began feeding instructions into the computer. Behind him, Sonny and Morgan turned to look down at the laser, attracted by the muted clicks of its flash lamp. They watched for about fifteen minutes before J.B. turned back to them.

"Got the idea?"

"Yes, but . . . nothing seems to be happening," Sonny pointed out.

J.B. smiled. "It's happening," he assured them.

They nodded, dubious, and J.B. laughed. "Well, just take my word for it. And go get yourselves a couple of beers. No use all of us staring at the computer."

He watched Sonny take the stairs two at a time, followed more deliberately by Morgan. Strange sort of guy, he thought. Maybe he's used to working alone. He turned back to the computer and called for a spectrograph. Morgan Curtis. Curtis Morgan. I'll never keep it straight.

Chapter 18

The day they started lasing, a tremor ran through Southern California. It registered six point two on the Richter scale.

"My God," whispered Arthur, drawing a chair closer to the TV set in the Club West. It seemed as if the magnitude of what they were attempting had finally dawned on him.

Sam threw up his arms. "Hallelujah!" he crowed. J.B. glanced at Pandora, but she was staring at the screen.

"Just think," Sam explained, "in one fell swoop—pardon me, lase—we wipe out half the kooks in the country."

"J.B.," Arthur said solemnly.

"Don't worry," J.B. said, still laughing at Sam's outburst, "it's got nothing to do with us. For one thing, we're going in the opposite direction."

Arthur sighed deeply, but he peered at the TV screen, overcome by the forces of nature whose handiwork was being traced on the evening news. Cracks a few inches wide in the desert outside Los Angeles, a house trailer tilting, broken dishes, no serious injuries.

"Aw, heck," Sam complained. "The chance of a lifetime, and we muffed it. J.B.," he called, jabbing a cigar at him as he headed for the kitchen, "I want you to rev that thing up and really let her rip."

J.B. smiled. He took a deep breath and let his shoulders sag as he exhaled. For the first time, he was beginning to feel relaxed.

He jumped at a loud pop from the kitchen.

"Here, kid," said Sam, "you first." J.B. took one of the glasses Sam was holding and watched him pour from a bottle of champagne.

"You've got a lot of class, Sam."

"Don't flatter me, kid, makes me nervous. But I thought we ought to have a little celebration." He circled the room, pouring drinks for all.

"Ah, yes," Arthur intoned, swirling the liquid in his glass, "August was a very good month." Bob giggled.

Arthur rose, hand outstretched. "I propose a toast: to Straight Arrow, and the man who will guide it on its way." J.B. hesitated as the others turned to look at him, then saluted them and took a gulp. He stared over the rim of the glass at each of them in turn. His glance lingered on Arthur, whose lapel was aflame, as a ray of setting sun caught the small medallion he always wore—a gold-colored eagle with some inscription in blue. A memento from the President's Club, no doubt, or his finance committee.

A fine bunch of crooks we all are, he thought, letting another sip slide down his gullet, feeling his stomach warm. Well, maybe it will all turn out all right.

Chapter 19

The following day, they put the laser down in the tunnel. Sonny and Morgan lifted it out of its cradle, and J.B. swept aside the support. Then the three of them set it on the tracks and eased it down into the shaft. It rolled in smoothly.

J.B. turned on the generator and the computer and typed a command. The laser disappeared, powered by a small motor that would keep it moving slowly as the beam vaporized a path.

Now that the laser was down, J.B. could set up the ruby laser that would monitor the direction of the shaft and allow them to measure its length. At the entrance to the tunnel he carefully arranged the small laser and the detector, with its photosensitive cell, each slightly offset from the center. He hooked them up to an oscilloscope, and wired all to the generator and the computer.

A few taps on the keyboard, and the curves of two amplified pulses of current appeared on the oscilloscope. "This first curve," J.B. explained, "is the pulse from the ruby laser hitting a mirror on the back of Straight Arrow. The second peak is the pulse that's reflected from the mirror to the detector." He pointed to the space between the two peaks. "From the width of this space, we can calculate the length of the shaft, but don't worry about that. We'll let the computer do it. The important thing—." He searched the table for a grease pencil and drew a circle around the display. "Is that this diagram should always appear in the same area on the scope. If it moves, that means we're off course and we'll have to make a correction.

"We've got another check over here," he said, turning back to the computer to feed in a command. A diagram of a circle divided into squares

61

came up on the screen. He pointed to the "X" near the center. "That's the laser. If it moves out of the circle, it's off course."

"How often should we check it?" Sonny asked.

J.B. pursed his lips. "A couple of times during a shift should be enough."

He tossed the pencil on the table. "I think that's it for now. We can start our regular shifts today. I'll look for one of you at four." They left, and J.B. settled back to let the laser get down to about eighteen hundred feet.

The slight hum of the generator was the only sound. Buried underground, he was cut off from any noise outside. Eerie, he thought. After a few minutes, he instructed the computer to begin lasing.

Slowly he became aware of a vague, scraping sound. He turned to look at the tunnel. The power cable and hoses were feeding steadily into the abyss, scraping the floor as they moved. Well, he smiled, there's one sign that Straight Arrow is moving right along.

Chapter 20

With the project underway, Arthur and Carl returned to Washington. The days settled into a routine. Working eight to four, J.B. felt like the average working stiff, and delighted in the experience. It was pleasant to be average for a change.

Morgan, calling himself a night owl, had elected to take the graveyard shift, and so it was he and Bob and Sam whom J.B. saw most often at dinner. Pandora appeared from time to time, but generally she stayed in her own quarters.

Alfie entertained them with stories of growing up in Gary, Indiana.

"It smelled bad all the time, man. You know, from the steel mills? We burned tires in the backyard so we wouldn't smell the smoke from the stacks."

Even Morgan smiled.

"Was it rough growing up there?" Bob asked. "I mean—you being Spanish, and all."

"No, it wasn't bad," Alfie allowed. "The Italian kids beat up the Irish kids, and the Irish kids beat up the Mexican kids. Just like your average American city."

J.B. traded stories with the rest of them—all except Morgan, who seemed to have been born in a vacuum somewhere in South Dakota—resuscitating his youth in Fort Worth. Those were good days, he thought now, riding in the hills and fishing in the Trinity River, long before the city had begun to grow upward and outward; although it seemed to him then he couldn't wait a New York minute to get away from all those dumb and boring people. So he had gone off to study geology in Colorado, cruised around Latin America for a while before going back to graduate school, and then he was on his own, ready to take the world by the horns. Well, he had certainly made a few waves.

As the weeks drizzled by, the appeal of camaraderie began to wane. Despite his having lived and worked in Washington—or was it because of it—Bob was less than stimulating. He lived on the fringes of power, content with a game of poker now and then with other low-level bureaucrats. Curtis Morgan—oops—was simply a dud. Of course, there was Sam, with his astringent tongue, but he seemed to contribute more growl and less wit as time went on. Maybe he was growing boring, too.

J.B. tried to remember that they were all here simply to do a job and get out. But two years, if that were all it took, stretched out before him like a life sentence. Well. Not quite like a life sentence.

He took to preparing his own meals and watching television. Steaks and chops still were a luxury, but they depleted his cooking repertoire. Soon he had turned the TV voice down to an incoherent mumble, just enough noise to remind him there were other human beings on earth. The solitude he had so much enjoyed in his first days at White Sands, after the sardine-can life at the pen, became oppressive in the desert nights.

Marybelle's face drifted in and out of his consciousness, drawing a frown. What kind of stimulation had he had with her? Hell. He had had Marybelle.

He hesitated when Bob one night invited him to dinner, then accepted. Maybe he was better in a one-on-one situation.

"I do terrific things with steak," Bob confided, and J.B.'s stomach sank, but the teriyaki did, indeed, turn out to be an agreeable diversion.

"How did you get to be the president's press agent?" J.B. wanted to know.

"Secretary," Bob corrected him, leaning back and savoring his wine. J.B. watched him expand, his nervous twitter gone. He was taller than he seemed in Arthur's overbearing presence, or even with the others, and there were lines in his boyish face.

"I went to school with the president," Bob began. "We were friends back in . . . sixth grade. I knew him when he was stealing hubcaps and copping feels." They both laughed.

"We kept in touch, and when he started running for office—state senator, governor—I got involved. I was his advance man when he started working toward the presidency."

"You married?"

Bob smiled into his glass. "Not anymore. Lila stuck it out for two months in Washington. Then she went back home with the kids." He looked up at J.B. "I couldn't leave. It was pretty exciting in the early days. So much happening, and you think you can really make a difference." He snickered and studied the glass. "I thought the president needed me.

"Anyway, you can't live apart for very long without things changing. We got divorced last year."

J.B. nodded and poured some wine into his glass. "You still feel needed?" he asked.

Bob chuckled. "Big shots like Arthur—they're always around, pushing. The pressure on the guy is terrific, you know? I get to say my piece once in a while . . . . Remind him of the days when he used to steal hubcaps . . . . Yeah, I think I can help."

"You're not exactly at the center of things, out here," J.B. reminded him.

"Well, I could use the vacation . . . . Hell, I needed to get away from that Washington crowd," he smiled sheepishly. "They're like a school of sharks," he confided. "They don't care what you're trying to accomplish . . . they just keep circling and waiting for you to make some slip, and then they pounce." His glass hit the table with a thump, but he ignored the spurts of wine that splattered on the table.

J.B. looked away. For the first time he noticed the photographs taped on the walls. In them, their cluster of trailers crouching beneath the mountains took on an air of historical authenticity. There were closeups of yuccas and prickly pear cactus with voluptuous cerise blooms, long shots of the scarred and shadowed mountains that flanked them, an endless expanse of grass, a jack rabbit sheltering behind a greasewood bush. This was not the dun-colored desert in which J.B. moved, but a home to an infinite variety of life and nuances of color and form.

"You're pretty good at this photography stuff, aren't you," J.B. marvelled.

Bob grinned. "I love it. It's been my hobby for years." He scanned the room. "Maybe I'll just go back to St. Louis one of these days and open a studio."

"What did you do before?"

"I had a PR firm there."

He rose and cleared the table, carrying the dishes to the sink. "How about you?" he called. "You ever been married?"

"No. I was always pretty much of a loner—for the most part."

Bob returned and sat down and studied him. J.B. could see the questions forming. "Why?" "How could—?" Not tonight, he thought.

"Well, I guess I'll mosey on back home. Thanks for dinner."

They shook hands at the door, and J.B. felt the man's eyes on his back as he trudged through the grass.

He dreamed that night of a yellow ribbon tied around an old oak tree, and broccoli crepes.

Chapter 21

"Pandora, I need a book."

"What book?" She stood holding the half-opened door, as if barring his way.

He frowned. "I don't know. What are people reading these days?"

She gazed at him doubtfully.

"Look," he pleaded, "I'll go crazy out here just watching that computer screen every day. I need something to keep my brain awake. Can't you get me some books? Any kind of books."

She blinked. "Sure, J.B."

"And a newspaper. How about a Washington paper?"

She nodded.

"I'm in limbo here . . . on the moon!" he emphasized.

She stared at him. "I'll see what I can do."

He hesitated, feeling his legs unable to move. He forced himself to turn. "Thanks," he called back.

The truth dawned on J.B. He yearned for the company of a woman.

* * *

She brought him books. And after a few weeks, the Sunday edition of the Washington Post began arriving.

"I'd like to see that Updike book when you're finished," she ventured.

"Sure. Of course. And thanks."

He devoured Updike and Stephen King and Tony Hillerman and Anne Tyler. A varied bunch. Pandora must have gone down the best-seller list, he decided.

He began to watch her trailer carefully, for those occasions when she sallied forth to dine at Alfie's. Then he hurriedly grabbed a clean shirt, waited a discreet few minutes, and ran out after her.

The conversation was no more scintillating than in her absence. But her appearance put a mild glow on the evening. Locker-room jokes were bypassed for polite inanities and a few harmless lies, and wine supplanted the usual beer. Alfie was as vulnerable as any of them to a woman's charms, and Pandora, cop though she was, lacked none of them.

Chapter 22

J.B. was almost relieved as the time neared to pull up the laser. At least it would provide a break in the routine, and enough physical labor to weary his body and put his libido to sleep.

They had begun drilling on May eighteenth. The tungsten-halogen flash lamp had a life expectancy of a thousand hours, or about forty-one and a half days. Just to be on the safe side, J.B. decided to bring up the laser after forty days. They would send it to Los Alamos for replacement of the flash lamp and for polishing.

On June twenty-seventh, J.B. shut down the laser. But before hauling it up, he took a last reading from the oscilloscope, instructing the computer to calculate the distance traveled . . . . Not too bad.

Sonny and Morgan helped him move aside the equipment in front of the tunnel, as he explained the procedure for pulling up the big laser. The motor would take it back at the cautious rate of twenty-five miles per hour. The winch, which they had noticed sitting off to one side of the chamber, would haul up the cables. But they would have to wind them up as the laser backed up.

Sonny and Morgan agreed to work outside, pulling the power cable and the air hose through the tunnels that had been dug from the laboratory wall to the desert surface, and winding them on spools. Down in the lab, J.B. kept the lines straight as they slipped off the drum of the winch, and wound up the computer cable. It took them nine hours.

Carl drove up in a cloud of dust the following morning, accompanied by Arthur.

"Who's minding the store?" J.B. asked, nodding in the direction of the defense secretary, who was marching toward his trailer.

"*Nobody*," Carl emphasized. "Everybody who can is taking off for the Fourth of July weekend. Washington is a blast furnace. Arthur and I decided we'd take care of the laser business and then stay on for the holiday."

Of course J.B. had been oblivious to the approaching Fourth of July. Now he felt a pang as the words called up images from the past. The holiday meant friends and comradeship, whether real or imagined, cold beer and warm potato salad. He felt more than ever like an exile.

Carl interrupted his thoughts. "Is the laser ready to go?"

"We brought it up yesterday."

"Good. Let me get Arthur. He wants to see it."

There was really no need to open up the assembly, and probably it was not a very good idea, but everyone claimed to be dying to see the prism, and J.B., too, wanted a peek.

They crowded into the lab as he opened the hinges at the sides of the assembly and, with Sonny, lifted off the top section. Everyone pressed forward.

"Christ, you're going to suffocate me," J.B. complained. But he was pleased with the looks of it when he removed the top part of the cooling chamber. Lying in the cavity of the cooling apparatus, it glowed pinkly.

"It's so small!" Arthur exclaimed, evaluating the three-foot length of the prism.

"Big enough, I guess," Sam said dryly.

J.B. and Sonny replaced the top sections and eased the assembly into the crate in which it had arrived. Then Sonny and Morgan carried it upstairs, trailed by Carl. "See you in two days, I hope," he called back.

Bob looked after him and then back to J.B. "Why does it have to be polished?" he asked, "And why can't you do it here?"

J.B. had unclamped the flash lamp and was turning it in his hand. He sat back on his haunches. "Well, there are certain inherent flaws in the crystal." They looked at him blankly. "We start out, you see, by growing a crystal of yttrium aluminum garnet. Or, the boys at Los Alamos grow it. The prism is formed from the crystal, and in the process, tiny scratches and pressure zones are introduced. As the laser operates, all these flaws are slowly magnified, and the efficiency of the laser diminishes. Polishing gets rid of some of these flaws and restores the laser's efficiency."

They nodded, apparently satisfied. He turned back to Bob. "As to Los Alamos, they've got the equipment to do the job; it would just be too much trouble to duplicate here, and we don't have much room to spare, anyway."

"Makes sense," Bob agreed.

Arthur slapped the arms of his chair and rose. "Very interesting, J.B.," he said, in a very uninterested voice. "By the way, how far have we gotten?"

J.B. rolled the numbers out slowly. "Two hundred twenty-three point two miles."

"We're on schedule then?" The figures obviously were meaningless to him. "Right on," J.B. assured him, slightly piqued.

Arthur bobbed his head and strode to the stairs, followed by the others. Pandora glanced back before disappearing up the steps.

* * *

J.B. had plugged in the flash lamp and kept it on. When Carl returned with the laser two days later, it was still working. He decided to let the laser run for forty-two days this time. If the first flash lamp lasted much longer, maybe they could extend the time.

They lowered Straight Arrow down the shaft the next day. At about six in the evening, J.B. started the generator. He fed the computer instructions and turned the operation over to Sonny. It was beginning to seem very ordinary.

Chapter 23

Alfie disappeared the next day.

The clan had begun gathering at the club in the late afternoon when they first noticed his absence.

"I thought I heard a car...." Bob began. But no one had seen him leave, or had any idea why he had deserted.

"Well," huffed Arthur, "that's rather inconvenient. It's getting close to dinnertime." His eyes flicked over Pandora, who turned innocently toward Sam.

"He'll probably be back in a couple of hours," Sam offered. "What's new at the sweatshop?" he asked, to pass the time.

Arthur lowered himself into a chair. "We're having some problems up on the Hill, getting funds for the MX missile."

"Of course," said Sam, "who wants those things rolling through their backyards once a month?"

"That's the *old* game plan," Arthur pointed out with exasperation.

"Well, the new one's not much better."

Arthur narrowed his eyes. "If I didn't know better, Sam, I'd think you were one of those silly-putty-headed doves."

"Naw," Sam chuckled, "everyone knows I'm just an old rooster."

By seven, Alfie still had not appeared, and Sam volunteered to broil steaks. When Arthur backed Pandora into a corner for a quiet talk, J.B. decided to help in the kitchen.

Alfie blew in in time for breakfast Sunday morning.

"Where've you been all this time?" Sam asked.

"The jeep ran out of gas."

"So what's new?" Sam commented.

To J.B. and Carl, Alfie confided he had bought fireworks for the Fourth.

"Fireworks?" Carl raised his eyebrows. "I thought they were illegal."

Alfie was incredulous. "You gotta be kidding. Man, this is New Mexico." He then went into an enthusiastic description of the equipment he had obtained.

"We need some entertainment out here," he concluded. "Everybody is so serious."

While the three-man operations team continued their lasing schedule, preparations were begun for the holiday. Carl and Sam rigged an awning on one side of the Washington Club West. Bob constructed a barbecue pit. Pandora caught the spirit of the occasion and announced she would bake an apple pie. They agreed to give Alfie a day off. Sam and Bob would preside over the barbecue.

Embarrassed by all the activity around him, Arthur offered to make a salad with his famous ranch dressing. He also generously suggested that Straight Arrow be put on hold Monday afternoon until the following day.

Bob had the fire going by four, fed with mesquite and dead cactus limbs he had gathered. The others began drifting out of their quarters, bringing chairs or blankets. Alfie had insisted on making margaritas, and by five they were like any jovial group of suburbanites, gathered for a cookout in someone's backyard. Looks like the nucleus of another retirement community in the Southwest, J.B. thought, surrounded by distant purple hills under a sky unbearably blue to any Easterner.

Alfie began bringing out his treasures at eight-thirty, as the departing sun flicked out tails of orange and crimson.

"What's this?" Arthur inquired.

"Looks like any decent Fourth of July," Sam answered, sipping his fourth margarita. "Don't worry, Arthur, we won't tell."

Arthur lifted his head and looked down his nose at Alfie's baubles, but he couldn't take his eyes off them. Alfie was planting rows and circles of tiny paper-skinned rockets in the dirt; tiny, that is, compared with Arthur's usual inventory. He lit one fuse. There was a prolonged whine, an arc of sparks stretching into the sky, and then a clatter of exploding firecrackers.

Now that he had everyone's attention, he lit a series of Italian streamers. Star after star flamed, each trailing sparks. Next he set off a few Roman candles. Stars of red, blue and gold blazed, died, then blazed again. His audience cheered and clapped. Alfie began to alternate and then combine the effects.

J.B. was mesmerized. What was it about fireworks that bumped the human spirit and sent it soaring, along with the trails of flame and sparks? It seemed to gather everyone together under a canopy of pulsing light. And yet the excitement was laced with, even heightened by, a touch of danger. Was it dread of punishment for having dared to rival the lights of heaven? Prometheus had lost his liver for giving fire to man. J.B. imagined he could smell the fumes of Hades.

It was the sulfur from the rockets, and it brought J.B. out of his reverie. Alfie was building up to a climax now. He set off a battery of Roman candles. They were hardly extinguished when he let loose a flight of rockets.

Over the racket, Sam bellowed. "Hey, Arthur, why don't you light one? It's not exactly like having your finger on the button, but you might get a vicarious thrill."

Arthur's mouth puckered in distaste, but he reached for the matchbook Alfie held out. He knelt, careful to keep his pants off the ground, and lit a fuse. There was a hiss, and the rocket shot upward, climbing two thousand feet in six seconds, and exploded in a concatenation of sparks and retorts.

Alfie followed up with everything he had, mingling rockets and candles and streamers. The sky was ablaze with a clutter of expanding universes, lazing outward.

Suddenly the whoosh and pop of the fireworks were pierced by a scream. A gaggle of jet planes streaked through the dying stars, then banked and came in low. Arthur stumbled back and gaped. In another instant, they were gone.

Sam came up behind Arthur and stared in the direction they had flown off. "Makes you feel secure, doesn't it? Your boys are right out there doing their duty, ever alert to the dangers that threaten the soft underbelly of New Mexico."

The telephone in the Washington Club West was ringing insistently.

"It's for you," Alfie said. Arthur took the receiver from him.

"Yes?" Sam watched him come to attention.

"Yes, Mr. President.... Yes, Mr. President.... Of course.... One of the boys just...." Arthur closed his eyes.

"Certainly, Mr. President.... Yes, sir."

He replaced the receiver with a limp hand and pulled out an initialed handkerchief.

"What's the problem?" Sam asked.

Arthur's usually stentorian voice was a low rumble, as he wiped his brow and hands.

"The commandant at White Sands couldn't reach me in Washington, so he called the president. They put the whole base on alert when they saw blips on the screen, and scrambled three jets. The commandant said he thought we were here for more serious purposes than setting off fireworks and scaring the hell out of the army."

Alfie lowered his eyes and crept off to the kitchen for a beer. "The army doesn't have a sense of humor," he mumbled. "Or patriotism!" he shouted.

Chapter 24

It was three in the morning, only two days after the Fourth of July celebration and one day after the Washingtonians had left, when the rapping woke him. It took a moment for the features to arrange themselves into the face of Morgan, looking uncharacteristically flustered.

"The temperature, J.B. It's up to around six hundred degrees."

J.B. hurried into his clothes and followed Morgan to the lab, zipping and buttoning as he went.

Morgan had shut everything down. J.B. went through the procedure methodically. Turn on generator. A hum crept into the silence. Turn on computer. Give command to start lasing. The cables began to feed into the hole. Maybe it was just a flaw in the thermocouple. The cables stopped.

J.B. called for a temperature reading from the lasing head: six hundred and ninety. Then the air hose: around five hundred degrees.

"Go see if anything's coming out of the air hose," he directed Morgan. He rolled a pen in his fingers as he waited. Maybe it was the air pump. They could fix that without having to bring up the laser.

Morgan returned. "There's dirt coming out."

J.B. took another temperature reading: seven hundred and forty degrees. He flicked off the computer switch. Damn. It had to be the cooling system.

"That's it," he said, rising. "We'll have to bring it up." He shut off the generator. The silence offended him.

It was hardly daylight when J.B. tapped on Pandora's door.

"Sorry to wake you up so early, it's the laser," he rushed on. "Something's wrong and we've got to bring it up. Can you get in touch with Carl right away? He'll have to take it back to Los Alamos."

"Of course. Let me get something on, and I'll get right over to the club."

"Thanks."

*   *   *

"Just looks a little grimy," Morgan observed, when he and J.B. opened up the housing.

"That's the point," J.B. nodded. He ran the tip of a finger over a mirror, and frowned at the dirt it gathered. The lens, the flash lamp, the outer wall of the cooling chamber were covered with dust, and dirty streaks that led nowhere. The leaking nitrogen, while boiling away, had condensed moisture out of the air, which had settled as frost over the innards of Straight Arrow. After the nitrogen was gone, the frost had melted, leaving only a dirty residue.

J.B. felt around the tube. He could find no rupture, no hole. Probably just a tiny pinhole, he grumbled to himself, but big enough to shut down the operation.

"It doesn't appear to be anything serious," Carl consoled him that afternoon. "Maybe just a defective tube. They can fix that in no time."

But J.B. was irritated. "There are problems enough with this project without having to worry about the damn cooling system."

"It's worked like a charm up to now," Carl pointed out. "Don't be greedy."

J.B. laughed. "You're right, I suppose."

"I'll be back in a couple of days, and then you'll be back in business," Carl assured him.

Chapter 25

Morgan was sitting on the trailer steps, long legs drawn up in front of him, when J.B. appeared three days later. J.B. looked around. "Where is it?"

"Beats me," Morgan shrugged. "I haven't seen Carl, or that buggy he drove away in."

Sonny walked up to them. "All set?"

"Let's take a look downstairs," J.B. suggested.

Two steps down the ladder J.B. ducked and scanned the room. No laser.

Pandora opened her door with a yawn and blinked.

"What's wrong?"

"There's no sign of Carl or the laser. We're supposed to be putting it down the hole again today."

She frowned. "He should have come in last night." She stared at the tracks meandering south, through the grass, as if expecting him to appear. "I'll call Los Alamos."

They trooped behind her to the big trailer.

Pandora put down the receiver and turned to the expectant faces. "They say he left yesterday afternoon. They're notifying the state police."

* * *

Carl waved to the guard at the exit from a compound at the Los Alamos National Laboratory and turned onto Diamond Drive, then took a left and headed out on Jemez Road. He snapped on the FM and settled back, smiling, recognizing the wood winds picking out the first faint fragments of Mahler's First Symphony. The fanfare of horns and the notes of a cuckoo were a pleasant contrast to the rational, though not necessarily sober, discourse of the evening before.

Rational, yes, but also disquieting. Jerry's friends from the theoretical division talked confidently about chaos, beamed over proofs of the quirkiness of life, while those in applied physics hinted of weapons to repel beings from outer space. It was one thing to have a seat on the cutting edge of science, quite another to have one's view of an orderly universe take a little jog before one's eyes.

Los Alamos itself was quirky. Pink corrugated metal buildings next to concrete tiers enclosing fountains, blunt rectangular towers and round ones . . . and everything built on the rim of one canyon or another rising hundreds of feet above plains where clusters of Native Americans still chanted and stomped through dances designed to keep the world in balance.

As deputy secretary of energy, Carl was nominally in charge of the laboratory, but never quite at ease in it. He, too, preferred a world in balance, an orderly, deliberate progression, refining, smoothing itself, its meaning unfolding gradually.

Now the road lay straight and sure before him. Hills parted to reveal the Rio Grande valley below, backstopped by the Sangre de Cristo Mountains. The slow melody with its somber undercurrent was quickening, the beginning of a bright new day.

He slowed for a stop sign. A blue Chevy pickup coasted into the rear-view mirror.

He turned, past the tourists emerging from cars at the entrance to the Tsankawi prehistoric ruins. Now the day was in full swing, the orchestra erupting into an exuberant celebration of life. The truck route merged with the two-lane road from the city of Los Alamos, and Carl remembered there had been a blue Chevy behind him the other day, on the ride up.

On his right, the trees fell away into a canyon. The road curved to the left, and he glanced up at the pocked, iron-colored wall of rocks thrown up by ancient volcanoes and gouged by wind and water. The music was hushed, expectant, before dropping into a mournful key.

A thump brought his attention back to the road. The blue Chevy filled the side-view mirror. A mistake, he thought. Perhaps he had, gazing at the rocks, wandered across the median line as the pickup tried to pass. The next thump was harder and he gripped the wheel to maintain control. A glimpse of a line of mouth almost curling into a smile, dark glasses under a western hat, all framed by long dark hair.

He accelerated, putting several yards between them, then braked as the road swung to the right. The pickup overtook him and rammed the left rear fender again, bouncing away after the impact. Carl floored the gas pedal, two hundred feet of straight road ahead of him. The pickup hung back, then, as the road curved leftward, swung across the median line and bore down on the wagon.

Carl felt the impact just behind the driver's seat. The back of the wagon fishtailed to the right and the car skidded to a stop on an overlook.

The pickup was turned around in the opposite lane. Frantically, Carl started the motor, scanning the road ahead of him, behind, as if searching for somebody . . . anybody. It was broad daylight and someone was trying to kill him.

The wagon backed onto the pavement and the tires grated as he stamped on the accelerator.

The rear-view mirror revealed an empty road for a second, before a patch of blue began gaining on him. Carl glanced over at the canyon before the road took a long curve to the left. The pickup was coming down the center of the highway. He considered braking as it came alongside, letting it go sailing on. But he had never been much good at daredevil driving. The pickup was moving up. Now Carl could see the cowboy hat. He struggled to hold the wheel steady, bracing himself for the next blow.

The pickup was almost abreast of him. Carl felt magnetized by the driver's face. Was he drunk? No. It was a cold sneer he saw before the pickup veered sharply and smashed into the left front fender.

The wagon spun off to the right . . . and onto level ground stretching out to enclose the canyon. A wash of hot, steamy air lapped over Carl. They had come down into the flatlands.

He sat, panting, as the pickup dodged an oncoming car and sped down the road.

Mentally he examined his body, then pulled a handkerchief from a pocket to wipe his brow. The door refused to open; he slid out the other side and limped around the rear of the wagon, his right leg stiff. The left rear light was smashed. The gray of the metal body showed through a gash along the mid-section. The crumpled front fender pressed against the tire.

Leaning on the hood, Carl breathed deeply. A dramatic riff of horns rose from the radio, followed by triumphant smashes of drums.

He leaned in from the passenger side, snapped the radio off and extracted the keys, and checked the locks on the doors. The crate containing Straight Arrow had shifted, but appeared undamaged. Taking off his jacket, he folded it over one arm, loosened his tie, and started walking.

About a mile away, three adobes squatted before the mesa on the right, capped with what looked like sets of black organ pipes. Heat rushed up from the pavement and he stumbled, caught himself and walked on. There was no answer to his knock at the first house. As he retreated, curtains parted in a window of the second adobe, and a child's face appeared briefly. A yellow dog lying in the shadow of a Ford pickup looked up as he entered the yard and yawned. The door opened before he could knock.

"I beg your pardon," Carl began, "but I've had some trouble on the road—car trouble."

Black eyes examined him calmly, without emotion. The man was in his fifties, short and squat like a Pueblo Indian, his hair tied into a club at the back, a red kerchief around his forehead.

"Come in, come in," he muttered, standing back.

"I don't want to bother you," Carl insisted, "just thought I might use your phone."

"Sit down, sit down," said the man, urging him into a chair at the kitchen table. A woman in a print dress brought him a cup of coffee. An older man and woman gazed at him from a couch against the wall. The child he had glimpsed through the window sat next to them.

"Thank you," said Carl. "I'm sorry to trouble you. If I could just use your phone . . . ."

"No trouble. No phone," said the man, extending his hand. "Tony Abeyta. This is my family." He waved the other arm, indicating the others.

Carl shook his hand and nodded at the others. He sipped the coffee, smiled at the boy staring at him. In the unhurried rhythm of the home, beneath a dim light bulb, it seemed ungracious to press on.

Minutes passed. Carl tentatively examined the room. It was immaculate, the mud floor gleamed. A poster of John F. Kennedy smiled from one wall. In a niche nearby, a plastic Virgin Mary contemplated the plastic flowers at her feet.

"You have a lovely home," he ventured. Tony smiled. "I wonder, if there's a phone nearby. Perhaps I could call someone to tow me."

Tony chuckled. "It's Sunday. No one at work. We'll go tomorrow and look at your car."

Carl looked around him. "You'll stay here tonight," Tony declared. "Then we'll see about your car."

The next morning, Tony drove him back to the wagon. He got out, circled slowly around the forlorn vehicle, grunted. From the tool box in the bed of the pickup, he selected a hammer. Ignoring Carl's look of horror, he proceeded to hammer the fender into a reasonable facsimile of its old self, then took his tools to the door. It opened with a creak. Tony nodded and smiled.

"I don't know how to thank you," Carl said, sensing that money was not the answer.

Tony was already climbing into the pickup. "Go in peace," he said, waving. "And next time, cover your ass."

* * *

"Someone tried to kill him?" The president was agape.

"Apparently," Arthur responded. "At least, someone tried to drive him off the road."

"Carl thinks it may simply have been a Sunday cruiser," reported the secretary of energy. "You know, one of those high-riders, or low-riders."

The president stared at him.

"Some of the, uh, natives," explained the energy secretary, "jack up their pickups so the bodies are several feet above the ground. Others set their cars down low, so they practically scrape the road."

"You mean Indians?" inquired the president.

"No, no, Mr. President," Arthur corrected him, "they're Spanish, or Mexican . . . ."

"Hispanic," said the energy secretary.

"Why?" asked the president.

"Why what?"

"Why do they do that to their cars, their trucks?"

The energy secretary shrugged. "I really can't say . . . ." He thought for a moment, then brightened. "Perhaps it's related to the male display of some animals, during the mating season."

The president coughed. "Do you think it was just a cruiser?"

The energy secretary glanced at Arthur.

"That's certainly a possibility," the defense secretary equivocated. "The natives—Hispanics—are not overly fond of Anglos. There was a case just recently, in fact, where one of them was claiming title to a piece of one of those old Spanish land grants, keeping the true owners, a development company from Arizona, I believe, at bay with a horde of relatives and shotguns."

The president's mouth was dropping again. Abruptly he closed it. "You don't think it could have been something more serious," he suggested.

Arthur drew himself up. "We have, of course, instituted the strictest precautions to assure the secrecy of the project. We have excellent security at White Sands, and at Los Alamos, as you would expect."

"And how is Carl?" asked the president, studying a point on the far wall above the heads of the two men.

"He's fine, Mr. President," replied the energy secretary, "he was just shaken up a bit. And of course he was distressed when the state police arrested him."

"They *what?*"

"Well, they misunderstood the situation, and thought he was stealing secrets from Los Alamos. They've been a bit touchy since that Howard fellow, the ex-FBI man working for the New Mexico legislature, defected to the Soviet Union."

Chapter 26

The question was: How to get invited to dinner by Pandora?

He could be direct, just march up and say he was starving for a good home-cooked meal. But that might be too presumptuous. And he certainly couldn't fault Alfie's cooking.

I know, I'll turn the tables. Invite her to my place, just for the company. She'll probably refuse and offer to make dinner herself. And if she happens to accept—well, then, she'll owe me an invitation.

He stretched. It was five after four. Where was Sonny? He was cramped from sitting so long. He felt as if the contents of his head had solidified.

"Sorry, I got hooked on a TV movie," Sonny apologized, clomping down the stairs.

"Always a pleasure to see you," J.B. smiled at him. "Have a good night."

Emerging into the coolness of the workroom, he replaced the trap door, smoothing the rug over it. If they ever wanted to do him in, they could just nail down the door, he mused.

You're getting morbid, Craddock. He opened the trailer door and inhaled deeply. Christ, it must be a hundred and twenty degrees out there. He took his hat from the peg and crammed it on his head. When he turned to the door again, Pandora was outside.

"Hi."

"Hi. I'm just leaving."

She thrust her hands in her pockets. "I thought you might like to come over for dinner tonight. It gets kind of quiet around here, doesn't it."

"You bet," he replied, trying to moderate his enthusiasm. "I'm getting tired of talking back to the television set—or to Bob."

She smiled. "Around six?"

"That'd be fine."

She walked off. Now that wasn't so hard, J.B. grinned.

He showered and shaved, then spent ten minutes selecting a shirt. He picked a navy blue one. Nice and sedate. Brushing his hair, he examined his image critically. Very respectable looking, he thought, especially with those damned slivers of gray.

On the way to her trailer, he took a detour to a patch of yuccas. Don't these things ever bloom when people are around, he wondered? He stuck his hands cautiously between the sword-sharp fronds to break off several dried blooms. He sucked in a sharp breath as one drew a thin red line across his finger. Clutching the bouquet, he walked back toward the trailer, whistling.

Pandora looked blankly at the cluster held out to her and then laughed. "I'll have to get out my prettiest vase for these." She found a tall glass for them, and set it in the center of the kitchen table.

"Sit down, why don't you."

J.B. sat. He felt as if his tie were too tight, except he wasn't wearing one.

He said little during dinner, and so did Pandora. You dummy, he thought to himself, now that you're here, say something, be charming, or she'll never ask you back.

"Um. Is there any more?"

"Of course," she replied, and ladled out more beef stroganoff for both of them. But mostly she seemed to push hers around the plate, glancing at him occasionally.

Finally he pushed his plate forward. "OK. What do you want to know?" he asked quietly.

Her mouth gaped. "Oh . . . . No. I . . . um."

"I killed her," he said, in the same tired, toneless voice. "I can't change that."

She hesitated. "You don't seem like the type."

"Maybe we're *all* the type."

She clasped her hands and leaned forward, elbows on the table. "I'm sorry, J.B. I don't mean to pry. I guess you've paid for it."

"Three years in the pen? That's nothing. A couple more, and I'd have been an animal, like the rest of them." He thought of Wild Bill Everett and Ché and closed his eyes, trying to shut out their images.

"What was she like?"

"What was she like," he repeated, eyes still closed, leaning back as he tried to conjure up Marybelle. He saw her come striding through the swinging doors of the Palace Hotel, past the bar where chairs swiveled as men, and not a few women, turned to follow the tall figure, her hair a streak of silver. Hands waved, a chair was found, and she was persuaded to join a table.

Sitting near the end of the bar, he had checked the door from time to time, waiting for Ben Holloman, but found himself returning to her. On the dance floor, she moved purposefully, aware of the glances she attracted, acknowledging none but her changing partners. Even the swirl of her long skirt seemed controlled.

A little flashy, he remembered thinking. He had never much cared for blondes. And yet she wore no lipstick, and only a narrow band of silver encircled one wrist.

She had seemed to be with no one in particular, and so eventually he had forced himself to court rejection and ask her to dance.

Large brown eyes moved up and over him, and then she smiled.

She was almost as tall as he, but she moved lightly, anticipating his steps. She was not beautiful, at least not as he had imagined; a slight bump interrupted the long nose, and the smile was a trifle crooked. But there was a playfulness about it, and a hint of challenge behind the eyes.

He had escorted her back to her table and retreated then, but a few dances later, he joined the group. They all worked for Broussard, a major supplier to the oil patch. He had nodded and smiled and answered an occasional question. By the time the lights came on and the band began to pack up, they were alone. He had gone home with her. The next day, he had moved in.

He opened his eyes. "What was she like?" Pandora had asked.

"She was an A-one bitch . . . and the most beautiful woman I've ever known."

Pandora stared at him, then looked down.

"Well," he said, pushing back in his chair and rising. "Time to go." He felt like a zombie, moving through some predestined ritual. When had he done this before?

"But I do want you to know how much I appreciated this." He held out his hand instinctively, then withdrew it. Still trying to rejoin humanity, he thought.

"I'm sorry, J.B. I didn't mean to . . . dredge up old memories for you." But her voice was flat, and she had drawn a screen across her face.

"I guess that's something I'll have to deal with." He turned toward the door, frowning. This was not how he had planned things. But then he had not planned to move in with Marybelle, or to kill her.

He thought of Ben Holloman, who had tempted him to the Palace Hotel to discuss a proposition, but had never appeared that night.

Yes, there were a lot of things he had to deal with.

Chapter 27

Sonny was late again, and J.B. was irritated. He had had his chance with Pandora and ruined it, he had not slept well, and he longed to crawl back to his den and hide under the sheets. Where was his relief man?

The memory of his first meeting with Marybelle had dislodged disturbing questions. Why *had* he killed her? Once it had seemed so simple. He had found her in their bed for the third time with another man. The first time, it had been a former lover, a Dallas lawyer with a wife and kids who, explained Marybelle, had insisted on seeing her for an innocent lunch, but things had gotten out of hand. Then there was the trucker she had picked up at a bar one night when he was working late. Why had she brought them home, instead of going to a motel? Each time he had not been expected home—at least not early enough to interrupt them in flagrant disregard of . . . of what, his pride?

No, fidelity was not one of Marybelle's more endearing qualities. Of course, they had never married. They had discussed marriage on occasion, but casually, almost impersonally, warily. Had he really wanted to marry her? Would she have married him? He had never asked.

But certainly theirs had been a meaningful relationship. What *was* the meaning?

He knew her breaches of fidelity implied no criticism of his own love-making. They came together exuberantly, feeding on each other's flesh until they were exhausted, and content.

What had she been trying to tell him?

And what was Sonny, that no-good hulk of an airhead, trying to tell him? He was forty-five minutes late now.

J.B. quickly checked the direction of the laser. The "X" floated serenely within its circle on the screen. Then he activated the spectrometer. Benzene. He grunted and tapped his fingers on the edge of the console. Another reading: benzene again. He waited five minutes. Benzene. Then a fingerprint of calcium carbonate. He drew a deep breath and shut down the laser.

He stomped over to Sonny's trailer and knocked on the door. There was no answer. He knocked again, harder. Probably working on a beer belly in front of the television set. The door was unlocked and he stepped inside, calling Sonny's name. The tick of a clock reproved him softly.

"They left right after breakfast," Alfie informed him. "Sonny said he wanted to take a look around, and Bob said he'd go along."

"Take a look around what?"

Alfie shrugged. "Some of the towns around here, I think. They took one of the four-wheel drives."

Great. J.B. set his jaw and trudged back to the lab. We're about to plunge into a pool of oil or some damn stuff, and he's off on a holiday. Of course, there was nothing Sonny could do to prevent such a catastrophe, but J.B. did not care to be mollified.

* * *

"I think we ought to go, Sonny," Bob repeated, but Sonny waved away his anxious words.

"What's the hurry? We haven't been off the base since we started this gig. It's about time we relaxed. Here," he insisted, pushing a glass in front of Bob, "have another drink." Bob wrinkled his nose at the tequila, as Sonny ordered another round for himself and his new friend. The man smiled, tossed down the drink and sipped his beer.

"Don't they give you guys any time off?" he asked. "I thought the army kept regular hours these days. How many missiles can you shoot, anyway?"

Sonny turned his back to Bob to answer. "Doesn't have anythin' to do with missiles," he explained, shaking his head and waving a very relaxed hand back and forth in front of his face. "No, sir, we don't have nothin' to do with missiles, or anythin' else that flies." He leaned toward the fixed gray eyes beneath the cowboy hat. "We're moles, Billy Bob," he whispered, "that's what we are."

He and Billy Bob had been taking turns buying shots of Herradura and beers for the past two hours, ever since Sonny had become bored with the circle of old men at the corner table staring at visions of their long gone ranches, swallowed by the army when it fenced off two million acres of dirt and cactus for the White Sands Missile Range. Billy Bob had been more friendly, offering them drinks at the bar. Now he signaled for another round.

"Sounds interesting—like some secret project," he was saying.

"It *is* secret," Bob interrupted, leaning across Sonny and speaking directly to him, "and it's time we got back to it."

Sonny ignored him, nodding toward a group of airmen sitting at a table. "While those flyboys are cruisin' around up there, we're down in the dungeon, Billy Bob, diggin' a hole, drillin' a lit-tle bitty hole you can't even see." He tipped the beer bottle up and gulped.

"Now tell me about this roundup," he said, poking a finger into Billy Bob's black leather vest. It had been the sign outside advertising the roundup that had lured them into the dusty little bar on the outskirts of Alamogordo.

"Oh, you know these cowboys, got nothin' to do for excitement, so they ride into the desert to catch rattlers. One who catches the biggest one wins."

"Doesn't sound like *you're* too excited," Sonny smiled, regarding the ellipses of checked cloth that rhythmically appeared and disappeared between the metal buttons on the straining vest. "I thought you were a cowboy . . . even with that Harley o' yours."

"Sure 'nuff," said Billy Bob, "but I got better things to do with my time," letting his eye wander back toward the young waitress planting beers among the tables. "So what are you drilling for . . . gold?"

Sonny snorted. "No, man, that's old hat. There are more important things than gold these days."

Billy Bob nodded. "So you got this pneumatic drill or something . . . down in a dungeon . . . ."

Sonny laughed and slapped the bar. "Wrong again," he said, leaning closer and dropping his voice. "Ya see, we got this death ray—like Flash Gordon!"

Billy Bob gazed at him above his glass, the gray eyes registering not the slightest emotion in the square face framed by lank brown hair.

Bob plunged into the momentary silence. "Look, Sonny, we've really got to get back. J.B. will—."

"Yeah, yeah, you're right," Sonny agreed, rising and falling into Billy Bob to shake his hand. "See ya at the roundup, pal."

"Sure thing," Billy Bob mumbled, pushing him carefully toward Bob, who guided him toward the door. Sonny waved to the circle of old men. "Good luck, you guys."

"Save it for yourself," one replied.

They struggled past the Harley-Davidson and into the four-wheel drive.

"Funny," Bob mused on the ride back, "wasn't there a motorcycle behind us this morning . . . on the way to the bar?"

Sonny shook his head. "Ya think there's only one in New Mexico?"

*   *   *

Sonny wavered above the ladder. "Uh . . . guess I'm a little late, J.B."

J.B. looked at his watch. "It's only six-thirty."

Sonny grinned and lurched down three steps before noticing that J.B. was not smiling. The spectrometer, after signaling a few more benzene molecules, was indicating the usual rock now, but J.B. was weary. He longed for a hot shower and a screen that displayed nothing more problematic than a TV sit-com.

Sonny tackled three more steps and clung to the railing. "I'm really sorry, J.B. The time just . . . got away from us." The railing appeared to be getting away from Sonny. He leaned forward into a half circle before pulling himself erect.

J.B. sighed and then planted himself at the bottom of the stairs. "I can't do this by myself, Sonny. I need someone who's reliable."

"I know, J.B.," Sonny bobbed his head. "And it won't happen again, I swear it. Now you just go home and don't worry 'bout a thing." He had reached out a reassuring hand, and now his body followed, arching gracefully for an instant before it realized it was in midair, and then crashing into the waiting arms of J.B.

He grunted as he hit the floor and moved his head out from under the wreckage. Pandora's face floated at the top of the ladder.

"I'm glad to see you boys are getting along so well together."

J.B. tried to extricate himself and gasped. "I could use some help down here."

Pandora pattered down the steps. Between her pulling and his pushing, J.B. managed to slip out from under Sonny, whom they propped up against the stairs.

"It wouldn't have happened," J.B. pouted, dusting his pants, "if you'd been keeping an eye on things."

"Right," Pandora nodded, turning to examine Sonny, "blame it on the woman."

Sonny moaned and opened his eyes. "What happened?"

"You!" J.B. accused him.

He ran his hand over his head, then felt his leg. "It's my knee, J.B., it goes out once in a while, that's all."

"I'm sure it does," J.B. murmured.

"Just give me a few minutes . . . then I'll take over."

J.B. laughed at the sprawled heap of muscle. "I don't think so, Sonny. I think you've—." Take over? J.B. dashed to the computer and turned off the laser. He returned to stand beside Pandora.

"Think we could get him up the ladder?"

Pandora surveyed the limp frame. "Let's give it a few minutes . . . . Some coffee might help."

Over Sonny's protests, they fed him coffee and then pushed and pulled him up the steps and over to his trailer.

Outside again, Pandora pondered. "Do you think we should get someone else . . . to replace him?"

"No, he'll be all right. Can't blame a kid like that for wanting to bust out . . . . Not much to do around here."

"How about you?" she asked. "I mean, how do you feel?"

"I'm OK. Just got the wind knocked out of me."

He chuckled at the memory of Sonny flying down the stairs. "Why don't you ask Morgan to come over about eight? I'll work till then."

She stopped and examined him. "You look like hell, J.B. I'll have Alfie make some soup."

Chapter 28

They were sitting across the table from each other at the Club West, poking at apple pie. Everyone else had drifted away. But J.B. didn't want to leave. Neither, it seemed, did Pandora.

"That was very . . . good of you, about Sonny," she remarked, looking up from her plate.

J.B. shrugged. "He's a good kid."

"I would have thought you'd be angry."

"I suppose I was, before he showed up. I had all this benzene showing up, and I was worried about that."

"Is it OK now?"

"I think so. Anyway, I don't think it's worth making a big fuss over. If you took him off the project, he'd just get a black mark on his record. Everyone has a right to go off on a binge sometime . . . don't you think?"

She was searching apple pie for an answer. "It depends on how much damage you do . . . ."

So he told her about Marybelle, about playing house, about how Marybelle had introduced him to C.C. Broussard, who had offered him a job. About finding C.C. in his bed that night, after he had missed the flight to Houston. It had always seemed to him he had missed the plane deliberately, letting the monotonous staccato of announcements cascade past his ears, while he tried to concentrate on his newspaper, knowing there was some reason why he should go home.

He did not tell Pandora how C.C. had almost zipped up his usually private part in his pants, as he struggled to absent himself from that dank candlelit room. Then there was only Marybelle, backed into the pillows, face white but composed.

93

"How could you? Why?" he had demanded.

"Oh, don't be such a big baby," she had said. "Things like this . . . just happen."

"To you, maybe, not to me," J.B. had retorted.

"Well, I couldn't offend your boss, now could I?"

"What about the others?"

She had moved forward onto her knees. "They weren't important. They didn't mean anything, J.B."

"Then why bother? And why couldn't you offend my boss? You don't mind offending me. How could you do that to me—screwing him—here!"

"You don't own me, J.B."

The quiet declaration had stunned him. He might have walked away then, but she had continued the counterattack.

"And anyway, someone has to do something to help us get ahead. If it were up to you, we'd be down in the oil patch grubbing for a living. How do you think you got this job, anyway?"

That's when he had lunged for her, throwing her down among the pillows, shaking her by the shoulders. She had twisted away and he'd grabbed her hair, pulling her back.

"After all I've given up for you," he shouted.

"What have you given up for me? You haven't given up anything. I'm the one who—."

He'd smashed one hand over her mouth and grabbed her by the neck with the other. Then both hands were around her neck and, eyes closed, he thought he was flattening a can of beer.

There was no sound other than the hum of the refrigerator in Club West. Then: "What did you mean about what you had given up?"

"I only took that rinky-dink job because of her. Sitting at a desk . . . staring at sales figures . . . . What kind of job is that for a grown man?" He looked up at her with a skewed smile. Pandora waited, expressionless.

"Well, I just wanted to be with her. I didn't care, really . . . . There was something about her, something magical . . . something wild."

Pandora squashed a cigarette in a remnant of apple pie.

"Thank you for telling me about her, J.B.," she said, rising.

"Is it that late?" He pushed back his chair. "Guess I got carried away."

"Yes," Pandora agreed softly. "See you tomorrow."

* * *

J.B. stuffed his fists into the pockets of his jacket and stomped homeward. Marybelle again. Still. When would she pack her bags and get out of his life for good . . . stop insinuating herself into every conversation with Pandora?

Damn fool, he thought. Did you think it was going to be easy? He felt himself steeped in the odor of the grave, forever shadowed by a shroud.

He turned at the crunch of footsteps echoing his own. Pandora came up to him.

"I didn't mean to startle you." A breeze nipped at her hair.

"What?"

"I said, I think it's your turn to cook. Maybe we could barbecue . . . something simple . . . ."

"Steaks. I'll get steaks. Tomorrow."

"Good night, J.B." She turned. In a moment she was gone.

J.B. began to laugh. He laughed all the way back to his trailer. And then he sat out on the doorstep and watched the moon come up over the knobs and humps of the San Andres Mountains. The moon was as eroded as the peaks, pock-marked and only about a third full. He watched it climb silently through a whiff of cloud, and longed to break through the quiet of the desert, the prison that he carried around him. He threw his head back, and after a few tentative yips, let out a long, lingering howl of pain and frustration and emerging hope.

The silence came forging back, eating up the last remembered ring of his howl, and he was about to get up when he heard the clank of a door from the direction of Sam's trailer, and the thud of a shoe hitting the ground.

Chapter 29

They were playing backgammon at Pandora's place. Or at least Pandora was. J.B. was screwing up his face.

"It's all the rage," said Pandora. "You were . . . incarcerated too long. This is what people are doing these days."

J.B. glowered. "Makes me sound like a piece of meat. Don't people dance anymore, or tell war stories, or make love?"

"Not on a military reservation," she said primly.

He looked up and beamed. "Let's go to town."

"What town?" she asked.

"You're right. Your turn."

She rocked the dice in her hands. "J.B.," she murmured. "What's the J.B. for?"

"Jim Bowie," he said in a low voice.

"Jim Bowey?"

"No, dummy . . . Boo-ee."

She pouted. "Sorry. I'm just a dumb cunt."

His head snapped up. "Don't say that."

She tossed the dice and moved. "Did your ancestors fight at the Alamo or something?"

"Hell, no," he said, scooping up his dice. "They hid in the outhouse when the Mexicans came through." He gazed over her head. "But dad always had a romantic streak in him."

"And you?"

He counted off the spaces silently. "Not me." He looked at her. "I'm a ring-tailed roarer. Half horse and half alligator. I can outjump, outrun and outfight any man in these U-nited States." He thumped his chest. "Whoo-eeee!"

Pandora collapsed, laughing, across the backgammon board.

Chapter 30

The camp lay immobile under July's heat, and beyond the mobile homes, the only discernible movement was the occasional nod of a yucca responding to a whisper of wind. Like their desert neighbors, most of the inhabitants appeared only in the evening, huddling during the day in their air-conditioned burrows.

Through the inferno J.B. moved contentedly. From eight to four he was Vulcan, fashioning treasures for the gods from his underground abode. Of course, like everything else, the forge had given way to a computer. Now with a few finger taps he manipulated the very stuff of the earth. At least, he hoped he was manipulating it, boring a tiny path through the plates beneath the earth's surface that shifted as unexpectedly as a sand dune, cannily avoiding the pitfalls of magma and other sticky substances that could suck a man down into oblivion. Alfie brought him lunch punctually at noon, always staring quizzically at the cables that snaked across the floor and down the hole, always intrigued by the pattern on the screen when J.B. took a spectrograph. J.B. reacted as if it were the most normal activity in the world, too mundane to require an explanation.

Relieved by Sonny at four, he did pushups in his trailer to get the kinks out, watched the evening news on TV, and made dinner plans. Sometimes he cooked for himself. Occasionally he joined the group at the Club West, where Pandora might or might not be dining. More and more often they had dinner together.

Their mutual suspicion seemed to have dissolved. He was learning how to behave with a woman again, feeling easy and, yet, somehow alert. She asked questions and seemed interested in the answers.

Once or twice she appeared at the lab. She watched him splice the coaxial cable from a new spool onto the tail end of the old.

"Do you have to shut off the laser when you do that?"

"Yes. But it's only for a few minutes." He worked quickly and soon the purr of the generator resumed.

She asked whether she could work the computer, and he showed her how to take a spectrometer reading. She was delighted when the pattern flashed on the screen. He laughed.

In fact, they simply enjoyed each other's company.

Chapter 31

"J.B.," she began one evening, "I have a confession to make."

J.B., who had been about to refill her glass, straightened up. She looked at him meekly.

"I have no idea how you're doing what you're doing."

He blinked and then laughed. "You mean the laser?"

"Yes."

He bent and poured sour mash into her glass. "Well, you know what a laser is, don't you?"

"Light amplification by stimulated emission of radiation," she pronounced.

"Very good," J.B. smiled, sitting down beside her on the couch. "Cheers," he added, clinking his glass against hers.

"Yes," she murmured, and took a sip. "But . . . how does it work?"

He drank thoughtfully and put his glass down. "Well," he began, turning toward her and resting his arm on the back of the couch. "We start with a bunch of atoms just milling around, no place to go."

"What kind of atoms?"

"Oh, they can be any kind . . . depending on your purpose. Chromium atoms, like in a ruby crystal . . . neon, nitrogen. In our case, we're using neodymium ions."

She sat back. "That's an atom?" she asked skeptically.

He waved an arm. "That just means it's lost . . . or gained . . . an electron."

Her brow furrowed but she nodded, leaning forward again, and a musky scent flaunted itself through his nose. He sniffed and went on. "Well, the atoms are in what we call the ground state, just waiting for something to happen—sort of like kids hanging around outside a candy store, waiting for the action to start. Once in a while an atom will jump up into an excited state and give off a little energy—maybe he's watching a pretty girl go by—but he falls back again into the ground state."

Pandora smiled and sipped. J.B.'s hand fell casually on her arm. He looked away, concentrating on his exigesis, while his thumb, seemingly of its own accord, rubbed along the flesh.

"Well, now," he continued, "the trick is to get all those atoms into the excited state. To do that, you usually need an outside power source, like an electric current."

Almost imperceptibly he moved his leg against hers. His fingers climbed to her shoulder, and he watched them, like a disinterested scientist. Pandora raised her hand to touch a streak of gray in his dark hair. He leaned over to kiss her shoulder.

"What happens next?" she whispered, as he kissed the tip of her ear.

"Umm . . . . The electric current pumps up the atoms . . . ." His tongue slid down the curve of her cheek, her throat. "Into the excited state."

"What?" she breathed. "I couldn't hear—."

He raised his head and they kissed. His tongue prodded hers, and she licked delicately at the inside of his lower lip. She drew away to kiss the corner of his mouth, his cheek.

"Go on," she crooned.

"When they're in the excited state, they start giving off bursts of energy," J.B. mumbled, unbuttoning her blouse. He imprinted a light tattoo of kisses down into her bra, while fumbling with her belt.

"That's called 'spontaneous emission,'" he added.

Pandora giggled. Eyes closed, she slipped her hand under his sweater, caressing his chest. She began pushing the sweater up. He twisted to pull it up over his head and she lifted her face to him as he turned back. She felt the atoms racing through her loins, giving off bursts of heat. She reached down to help him pull her pants down past her knees.

"Then what?" she panted.

"Then the bursts of energy stimulate the atoms, keeping them pumped up . . ." His hand brushed the inside of her knee and grazed her thigh. ". . . until there are more and more of them racing back and forth, building up the excitement . . . until they're racing around together, all in phase . . . ready to burst at the same time in one continuous wave of radiation."

Pandora raised her body to meet him. She felt the whirling atoms crowding her loins, racing into line after line of compressed energy building up until they were moving in phase with J.B.'s atoms. Her body undulated with his, storing up more and more energy, until there couldn't possibly be any more. And then she let it out in wave after wave of coherent radiation.

And that's how Jim Bowie Craddock got into Pandora's Box.

Chapter 32

J.B. opened the door of the trailer and flipped his hat toward the desk in the corner. It missed. I knew it, he scowled.

He really hadn't meant to get involved with Pandora. He was here for one purpose only, to buy his freedom. He didn't want attachments with any of these people. A little pleasant conversation, some companionship through the long summer nights, was all he craved.

He climbed down the stairs and threw Morgan a sour "Morning." Morgan eyed him coolly. "Have a bad night?"

J.B. felt as if he'd been caught with his hand in the cooky jar. Then he relaxed. Hell, Morgan wasn't the cop.

"Sorry," he smiled, "just a little tired, I guess."

Morgan clapped him on the shoulder. "It does get a little tiresome. See you tomorrow, chief."

He let the hum of the generator settle into the back of his mind. He took a spectrometer reading. The pattern was comforting in its linear configuration, far from the kinks and quirks of humankind. Then he found himself doodling and staring at the name "Pandora." He sighed and dropped the pencil.

She didn't appear that day (he had forgotten she hardly ever did), and J.B.'s anxiety increased. Maybe she's taking herself off the job. Hell, what did they expect? They should have known better than to assign a beautiful woman as his jailer. He frowned. Maybe they had planned it that way. Maybe they wanted him to fall in love with her, to keep him tractable, content with lasing away his days and fucking away his nights, instead of plotting an escape. Nothing like a little woman to keep a man in harness. He remembered Marybelle, waiting for him—most of the time—when he came home late from that crummy desk job in Kilgore, reading a romance novel in bed.

He switched off the computer and the generator, and went upstairs. Not today. Today I'm taking myself out of harness.

He threw open the door and almost walked into Bob. "I'm taking the day off," he yelled over his shoulder.

"Great!" said Bob, hurrying to catch up with J.B., who was striding into the desert.

Suddenly he turned. "Did they send you to keep an eye on me?"

"Who?" Bob was perplexed.

"Never mind," J.B. answered, turning. He walked straight out for about a hundred yards. Then he sat down on a low hill. Bob sat down beside him. After a few minutes, he asked, "Anything I can do?"

"No," J.B. replied, his anger drifting away with the waves of heat radiating from the earth. "Thanks."

* * *

Sonny knocked on his door at four. "What happened, J.B.? Why is everything shut down?"

"We had a blueout."

"A blueout?"

"That's when the help doesn't feel like working." He pushed back his hair. "You can turn it on. Everything's all right."

He was back at work the next morning, whistling as he turned the corner of the laboratory and saw the piles of vaporized rock brought up by the air pump. He envisioned himself, down in the lab, being buried under the debris. And wouldn't some geologist, years from now, have a field day, trying to figure out how this strange sediment had found its way to the middle of a New Mexico desert?

At ten the trap door opened a crack and she peered down.

"Hello! Are you down there?"

"No. I'm cruising the Mediterranean."

She padded down the stairs.

"Missed you yesterday," he said, examining cable unwinding from a spool.

"I stayed in." She sat down in the chair. He said nothing, busying himself with unnecessary work, waiting. "I . . . didn't expect that to happen. It wasn't very professional."

"Oh?" He turned, looking at her for the first time. "I thought that was part of the plan."

She reddened. "Are you telling me I seduced you?"

He sat down on the floor a few feet from her. "No," he said quietly.

"There wasn't any plan. It—just happened."

He looked away. "Sorry?"

"No." She laughed. "A little surprised."

He turned and reached over to squeeze her knee.

"J.B.," she said, her voice low, "we'll have to be discreet. If they knew, they'd probably pull me off this case."

He let that one slide. So now I'm a case, he thought.

"Actually, they'd probably love it. Haven't you ever heard of Mata Hari?"

"I'm serious, J.B." She ran her finger up his hand. "Why don't you come over a little later tonight . . . about nine?"

Chapter 33

J.B. glanced out the window at the gray light and rolled back, clasping his hands beneath his head. Plenty of time yet. He stared up at the pocked white squares of the ceiling and thought of Pandora's creamy white skin. He closed his eyes and saw her face, swimming in a sea of red. He smiled.

Ah, how love creeps up and floods the soul with warmth.

That's not your soul, J.B., J.B. said to himself. Tell it like it is.

OK, so I've been three years without a woman, and now Maureen O'Hara with a cop's badge has allowed me to penetrate her inner sanctum.

Who's Maureen O'Hara?

Don't be insulting. You're as old as I am.

Yes, and beginning to feel the ravages of age—your age.

Nevertheless, this beautiful creature has brought a ray of light and hope, a new peace of mind, into my life.

She's a new piece, all right. That's what's wrong with you, J.B., always thinking sex is love.

Isn't it?

That's what got you into trouble with Marybelle.

I loved Marybelle.

You love tits and ass, buddy boy, and she was giving it away to every comer.

J.B. scrunched down in the bed and closed his hand around his penis.

Don't call me boy, he muttered.

Chapter 34

"She's having an affair?" the president gasped. "With him?"

"That's what Sam thinks," said Arthur.

"How does he know?"

"He says they ignore each other whenever someone else is around." Arthur smiled.

"It's . . . obscene."

Arthur strolled to the window to gaze out over the capital. "Actually, I think it's rather fortuitous. He'll be meek as a mouse—do just what we want and not make a bit of trouble." He turned back to the president. "Nothing like a woman to keep a man in harness."

The president shook his head. "And how is the project going?"

"Very well, Mr. President. I believe we're somewhere underneath Texas. Or maybe it's Louisiana."

The president was impressed by this display of precision. "Well, I hope it's not Cuba," he said dryly. "I trust he won't come up under one of our nuclear-armed submarines."

Arthur's eyes opened wide. "Hmm," he mused, "maybe that's just the sort of excuse we've been looking for . . . ."

Chapter 35

J.B. lit a cigarette and rolled back in the bed. He stroked Pandora's thigh.

"Lord. I think I've died and gone to heaven." She covered his hand with hers.

"Pandora," he pronounced. "How'd you get a name like that?"

"I thought it sounded mysterious. And a little sexy."

"A lot sexy," he corrected her, kissing her shoulder. "What's your real name?"

She removed her hand. He waited. "Well?"

She turned her back to him. "I'm not supposed to tell."

He considered that as he flicked the ash off his cigarette. "Pretty weak," he concluded. "Is it that bad?"

She turned back, rising up on one elbow. "You won't laugh?"

"I can't promise."

She screwed up her face and mumbled.

"What?"

"Dora Kronk," she said in a small voice.

"What?" he asked again, loudly now.

"Shh! Dora Kronk. And don't make me say it again!"

He smiled. "I think it's charming. But it doesn't really suit you." He raised up to kiss her. "Where you from, Dora?"

She sighed. "Boone, Iowa."

"Where's that?"

"You're full of questions tonight," she complained.

"I don't know anything about you . . . the unimportant stuff, that is."

"It's north of Des Moines. Daddy had a hardware store there."

"And you played with the nuts and bolts, dreaming of becoming a spy," J.B. rhapsodized.

"Actually, I dreamed of being a secretary. I went to Washington after school, and got a job with a lobbyist."

"How'd the CIA get to you?"

"I never said I was with the CIA," she protested.

"All right," J.B. smiled. "How did 'they' get to you?"

"My boss introduced me to someone. We went together for a few months . . . . He recruited me."

"And the two of you spied happily ever after."

"We're not all spies," Pandora said distastefully.

"What happened to him?"

Pandora gazed at him for a moment and then looked away. "He disappeared," she said matter-of-factly.

J.B. pondered that, and thought about a redheaded kid in Boone, Iowa. Then he rose and reached for his pants.

"I'm going to disappear, too," he whispered. "But I'll be back."

Chapter 36

It started as a mild hum, just as a blush crept shyly along the ragged peaks of the San Andres Mountains, as if someone had turned on a generator to light the day. The hum became a rumble and then thunder. Thunder? It was another gorgeous day dropping like a pearl into this rather desolate Eden.

J.B. sat up and parted the curtains of the tiny bedroom window. Nothing. He pulled on his pants and hurried outside.

Over the dun-colored slopes, down through a myriad of crevices, through clouds of dust, streamed men and boys and an occasional woman on horseback, dislodging clatters of stones, and now adding yips and whoops to the roar of hundreds of hooves pounding the ground.

Sam came staggering over to Pandora, who stared at the invasion. "What is it? Who are they?"

She shook her head, continuing to stare, as if, by a look alone, she could repel the strangers. J.B. reached for her, but as they neared the trailers, the riders veered around the encampment and spread out onto the plain, joining, as he now saw, riders pouring down slopes farther north.

A whoop behind them spun them around. Sonny was grinning. "It's the roundup!" he cried.

"What roundup?" J.B. demanded.

And as if in response, a rider slowed to scoop up a floppy object with a long hooked implement.

"Oh," said Bob, who had finally joined them for comfort, "yes . . . the rattlesnake roundup."

"Would you care to expand on that?" Pandora inquired.

"Well," Bob began, feeling as if he'd been accused, "that bar we went to near Alamogordo, they were advertising a rattlesnake roundup. That's why we stopped."

"The one who catches the biggest snake wins, something or other," Sonny added, looking yearningly at the riders. "Boy, I wish I had a horse."

Pandora crossed her arms and chewed her bottom lip. "They'll probably be gone by sundown," J.B. offered. "There's nothing much they can see."

"But how did they get here, J.B.? This whole place is fenced, there are guards, patrols . . . ."

"Pair of wire clippers, probably, in the middle of the night . . . ." They shared a conspiratorial glance.

"Mmm," she responded. "I guess I'll just keep an eye on them." She turned to the others. "But we shouldn't make ourselves accessible to them. I suggest we stay inside as much as possible."

Bob quickly agreed. "Fine with me," said Sam. Only Sonny lingered before turning toward the Club West.

They watched from the trailer windows for a time, although there was not much to see besides horses turning and backing and riders slapping at the ground amid spurts of dust, in some primeval dance.

"What do they do when they catch them?" Bob wondered.

"Put them in those gunny sacks they've got tied to their saddles," Sonny explained. "See?" He pointed as a rider plopped a snake into a sack.

"Can't they bite, through the sack?" Bob worried.

Sonny shrugged. "I don't know . . . I really can't say I'm that familiar with rattlers . . . or catching them. But it sure looks like a kick."

By afternoon, the crowd of riders had thinned, and there were fewer peeks out the windows.

The riders were gone the next day, as J.B. had predicted. Pandora scanned the hills with binoculars. Not a sign of life. She sighed and swept the plain . . . and stopped. About three-quarters of the way across, to the northwest, there was a shack. She frowned. Had that been there yesterday? Last week? Then horses moved into view. Time to saddle up.

Sonny offered to accompany her, and reluctantly she agreed.

"Now we're just going to take a look, Sonny," she admonished, "we don't want to start any trouble."

"Hey, no problem," he assured her, trying to keep his hands on the steering wheel as they bounced over the gnarled land. "I'm cool."

"Then slow down, please."

"Yes, ma'am," he grinned. "Maybe we could trade this in for a couple of horses."

"Or a wagon," Pandora suggested, from beneath the binoculars. "How do you suppose they got that thing down here?" she marveled.

Actually there were two wagons flanking the tiny wooden cabin, which still lacked a roof, a lack that half a dozen men were correcting by nailing sheets of tin over the pitched two-by-fours. Others were carrying cartons of pots and pans and sacks of beans and flour inside. Three men stood beside the door holding shotguns.

They watched silently, as the four-wheel-drive slowly came to a stop. There was a blink, a raised eyebrow, as Pandora emerged. They stood examining one another.

Pandora hooked her thumbs in her belt and took a few steps forward. "Morning," she nodded.

The man in the center smiled. "Mornin', ma'am."

She glanced from side to side and up at the roof. They were mostly old men, gray and slightly bent, thin and sunburned under their hats. A couple of younger men gazed down from the roof, mouths sprouting nails.

"Why, hello there, oldtimer," Sonny said, offering his hand to the man in the middle with his ever present grin. They shook hands all around.

To Pandora's look of surprise, Sonny responded, "We met these boys at that bar near Alamogordo, Bob and me." He turned back to the oldsters. "Had a few drinks together, didn't we?" The men chuckled and shuffled their feet. Sonny indicated the man in the middle. "This here's Jack . . . right?" The man nodded, then spat to one side.

"Well . . . what are you doing here . . . if you don't mind my asking?" Pandora ventured.

"This here's my land," Jack declared.

"Yeah, you said you'd take it back some day," Sonny recalled.

"But . . . this all belongs to the government now," Pandora objected.

"Not by a long shot," Jack retorted. "And who might you be, ma'am?"

"I'm . . . from the base. We both are."

Jack spat again. "The feds send you to do their work, did they?"

"No." Pandora stuffed her hands into her pockets. "Not exactly . . . we just thought we'd find out what was going on."

Jack leaned forward, hands on the barrel of the upright shotgun. "What's goin' on is, I'm takin' back my land, this land that the gov'ment stole from me thirty-odd years ago. And I'm not movin' this time."

She took in the nicotine-stained, arthritic fingers, the gray chin stubble, the eyes bright in the creased face.

"Well, thank you for your time . . . Jack?"

"Jack Hackleberry," he responded, and he spelled it for her.

She nodded and turned toward the truck. Sonny followed. They drove away to the ring of "Y'all come back now, y' hear?"

A jeep bearing two army men arrived at the Club West a few hours later to consult with Pandora.

Major Henry Graf listened intently, letting his coffee cool, staring out the window, grunting periodically. Lieutenant Timothy Jenkins took notes.

There was little to tell. Perhaps a dozen men, most of them old, about the same number of horses and two ancient wooden wagons. Definitely three shotguns. A tin-roofed shack some twelve-feet square that had mushroomed in the night. Food . . . but they couldn't have brought in much in two wagons loaded with building materials.

"I guess they took advantage of the rattlesnake roundup to come in; the dust was unbelievable," Pandora concluded.

"Rattlesnake roundup?" the major asked. Pandora explained.

Another grunt. "One small missile grazing their heads and they'd probably run for home."

"They think it is their home," Pandora reminded him. "At least, Jack Hackleberry does." She wondered about the women who had lived on that land; were their faces as creased and sunburned now? Were they dead? Had there ever been a pansy or petunia blooming out here, in a windowbox, or kitchen garden? Hard to think so.

"They were paid for that land . . . years ago. And more than it was worth," the major assured her. "The whole range couldn't have kept meat on the bones of three cows, if you ask me."

"Mmm." It was Pandora's turn to comment without commenting.

Major Graf tapped his teeth with a thumbnail. "One truckload of men could move them out in five minutes."

"Sir," the lieutenant put in, "it might not enhance the army's image to have a confrontation with a handful of feeble old men."

The major sneered. "PR. Yes. The new army specialty."

He rose and circled the carpet, hands clasped behind his back.

"But who put this idea in their heads?" he asked suddenly, pointing at Pandora. "Bunch of commies behind this, always is." He nodded at a deer peering out from between golden aspens on the wall. "The media would love to get their hands on this," he confided.

The lieutenant rose to face his boss. "If what Pandora has told us is true, we could simply starve them out. Wait until their supplies are exhausted. Patrol the perimeter and intercept any food being brought in . . . . Keep them under surveillance."

A final grunt. "Lay siege to them . . . . Yes." Disappointment washed his face as he reached for his hat.

To Lieutenant Jenkins he said, "I want to have a look for myself. We'll drive out that way."

"We'll be in touch," he advised Pandora.

"A pleasure, ma'am," smiled the lieutenant.

* * *

A persistent staccato sound tugged at J.B. as he left Pandora's trailer the following morning. He looked up to see a helicopter inching in the direction of the new boys on the block. Ah, yes, the army was conducting surveillance of the enemy. He ducked his head. No one was likely to recognize him from that altitude, but he felt like a jack rabbit in someone's sights.

When he emerged from his own trailer an hour later, after a shower and breakfast, he was pleased by the stillness of the land that he had come to think of as monotonous. Down to the sweet swish of the cables, the tiny clicks of the keyboard. They were all the noise he desired.

Chapter 37

On Friday evening, the clan gathered at Club West. Not that a Friday signified much here in the desert. It was a seven-day work week for the men assigned to Straight Arrow. But Sam believed in maintaining the rudiments of civilization even in this outpost of empire, down to the Friday evening cocktail hour and gathering of chums; Bob complied out of habit, and the others welcomed the ceremonious marking of time.

Besides, this was not an ordinary Friday evening. The invasion of the outlanders had cemented their sense of community. It had been one week since the cactus barons, as Sam dubbed them, had reclaimed their birthright. Or at least Jack whatever-his-name-was had. There had been no sound or sight of them since Pandora's visit, and no further word from Major Graf.

Lieutenant Jenkins, however, apparently also appreciated the weekly ritual. A knock at the door, and he was suddenly among them, smiling all around. Pandora introduced him.

"Well . . . what news do you have?" Sam asked.

"None, I'm afraid. They haven't really done anything. They finished the roof on the shack, and now they're just sort of . . . there. We see them patrolling the place, cooking."

"Isn't the army going to *do* anything?" Bob demanded.

"Not at the moment," the lieutenant replied, accepting a drink from Pandora, who ignored a stare from J.B. "We don't expect them to remain there very long."

"How long?" Sam asked.

"We estimate they might have brought in enough food for two, perhaps three weeks. After that, I think you'll start to see them drift back to

Alamogordo or wherever they came from. We'll let them go peacefully . . . but prevent anyone from coming in with food."

"Hmm," Sam smiled, "you didn't prevent them from coming in in the first place."

Jenkins blushed. "That really was quite unexpected. But now, of course, we've beefed up security."

"Soup's on, folks," Alfie called.

The lieutenant glanced at Pandora, who glanced at Sam and then, grazing J.B., called to Alfie.

"Do you suppose we can accommodate a guest for dinner?"

"Sure thing. I'll set another place."

"Will you join us?" Pandora asked.

The lieutenant pulled his six feet out of the chair in an instant. "Thank you."

At the table, he drew a chair out for Pandora and sat down beside her. The others distributed themselves around the table, J.B. at a far end.

"Actually," mused Morgan, passing rolls, "I don't suppose there's a security system in the world that can stand up to someone determined enough to get through it."

Jenkins frowned. "You're probably right." He buttered a roll thoughtfully. "The important thing, though, is how you respond to a breach—and how quickly." He smiled at Pandora. "Thanks to Pandora here we got right on it."

"Yes," Sam drawled, "about twenty-four hours after the cowboys came in." He added quickly, "Tell us about this Jack fella."

Chagrin gave way to gratitude as Jenkins recounted the history of Jack Hackleberry, native of Carrizozo, whose family had ranched in the Tularosa Basin, the great trough separating the San Andres Mountains and the Sacramentos to the east, since before New Mexico became a state in 1912. The federal government had tried to buy out the Hackleberrys in the early fifties, when it began putting together the jigsaw puzzle of holdings that eventually comprised White Sands Missile Range. The Hackleberrys, however, had refused the government's offer, and the money was sitting in escrow, the interest growing as surely as the resentment of the Hackleberrys, whose land simply had been condemned.

Jack, the youngest son, had been particularly angered by what he considered the expropriation of his patrimony. Apparently he was one of several ranchers who nursed their ire in the local bars with alcohol and dreams of redemption.

"Yeah," said Bob, "that's what they were doing, all right, when Sonny and I saw them."

"Sonny?" the lieutenant asked.

"He's another member of our team," explained Pandora. "He's working at the moment." The lieutenant waited, but no further explanation emanated from the team.

"I suppose they were offered a good price," Sam suggested, sounding unconvinced.

"It was eminently fair, I understand," Jenkins assured him.

"I'd have taken the money and run," Bob laughed. "Though I guess people get attached to their land ... even if it's just a few acres of rattlesnakes."

"Yes," Jenkins agreed. "Major Graf thinks they may have cooked up that roundup as a subterfuge, so they could slip onto the range."

"There are conspiracies all around us," Sam allowed, watching his thumbnail carve a ragged track through the label of his beer bottle.

The lieutenant cleared his throat. "Well. I don't really hold with conspiracy theories. But that certainly provided a convenient opportunity." He let his attention skip around the table and linger on J.B., who appeared to be concentrating on his dinner.

"How long have you been at the base?" Pandora inquired, drawing his attention back to her.

"Oh, just about three years." It was probably the best assignment he'd had, he added, fairly uneventful—he glanced at Sam—with time for him to continue his education and travel in Mexico. He had three degrees and was about to acquire a fourth, in philosophy.

"Of course, it's mostly a lark," he explained to the raised eyebrows, "but the army does afford many opportunities .... I've thought about teaching, after I retire."

Pandora nodded, and his gaze drifted toward J.B.

"Pardon me, Jim, but you look so familiar. I can't help thinking we've met."

"Don't think so," J.B. mumbled into his glass.

"Have you been in the army?" Jenkins persisted.

"No," J.B. lied. "I seem to have come along too early or too late for all the good wars."

"What are your other degrees in?" Bob wanted to know.

J.B. took advantage of the recitation to excuse himself. He caught the tail end—"criminology"—as he closed the door behind him.

He stomped toward the mobile homes, muttering. "Criminology.... Criminal, all right.... Where does the guy think he is, on some Ivy League campus?" As if to emphasize the point, his boot slipped off a clump of grass, and he stumbled. He righted himself and stopped. A long sigh, then a look around. Of course there was no one around to see him falling over himself.

A shadow took a jog at the corner of a trailer. He blinked, and instantly the scene rearranged itself.

Now I'm seeing things, he thought; I knew that guy was going to be trouble.

He picked his way carefully to his destination.

She found him in her bed, behind the red ash of a cigarette.

"Philosophy," he scoffed. "Can you believe that? Those guys have no sense of proportion."

"I think he's very well proportioned," Pandora countered.

"I mean, what's he studying, the philosophy of death and destruction? Rape and pillage?"

"You're awfully self-righteous."

He drew the sheet up over his exposed chest. "I could tolerate them better if they were honest. They're in the business of making war."

"Some of them think they're in the business of defense."

"Words to die by."

She stepped out of her pants and snapped the light off. "Jealous?"

"... Yes."

Chapter 38

That week they shot down the helicopter. It was invading their air space, Jack Hackleberry explained to a purple Major Graf, hovering just above their heads, making them nervous.

The pilot was not injured. The army retrieved him and abandoned the field to the cactus barons.

After his fury had waned, reported Lieutenant Jenkins to Pandora, Major Graf decided the incident demonstrated the frustration of the ranchers. They were expressing rage at the hopelessness of their situation. The army was wearing them down, refusing to confront them and provide them with an occasion for singing their cause to the media, or even to go down in a manly defeat. He predicted they would be gone in a matter of days.

And would Pandora care to go to a movie with him, the lieutenant?

Well, she really had things to attend to, she couldn't just leave at a moment's notice.

How about Friday night? Perhaps she could get away for just a couple of hours for dinner.

Pandora reluctantly agreed.

* * *

"Well, it's better than having him sit around here staring at you, or asking questions," Pandora reasoned. "You said you didn't like the way he looked at you."

J.B. sulked. "It'll just encourage him, and he'll hang around even more."

J.B. had a soft spot in his heart for the old men sitting outside the shack with their shotguns a couple of miles up the range, standing off the army but hardly ever seeing the whites of their eyes. It was poor land, dry land. No one could ever have dredged a good living out of it. But it was their land. There was a way the sun had of creeping up behind the hills in the morning, slowly revealing the slopes and valleys, separating the twisted bushes and plumes of grass from insubstantial air; pausing for the twittering gossip of the birds, and then exploding into a new day. Then creeping off at night under a crown of fireworks, trailing a robe of purple shadows.

Strange that a city boy could appreciate the attachment to such a land. Maybe he had seen too many westerns. Certainly there were some among them who simply hadn't gotten the price they wanted.

And certainly they were not all innocent victims. He knew of the range wars that had plagued the Tularosa Valley and environs in the late nineteenth century and the first decades of the twentieth. The daddies and granddaddies of some of these men had fought farmers and sheepherders and one another for the land, ridden against Billy the Kid, lined up for and against Albert Fall before he gave up on ranching and went on to make a name for himself selling leases to oil-rich federal lands for bribes.

But these were the remnants of those battles, stubborn men who persisted in the only lifestyle they knew, ornery men who hung on to their prejudices, men who now were fighting the federal government for the range—and had already lost.

He had a soft spot for them. But he wished they'd take their battle back to town, and with it, that overeducated, snooping, would-be seducer, Lieutenant Jenkins.

* * *

On Friday, there were isolated shots from uprange. A call from Pandora brought out a team of fresh helicopters, careful to cruise above the range of a shotgun.

"Apparently, they're just after game," Lieutenant Jenkins reported to the group assembled at Club West that evening.

"What can they possibly find to eat out here?" Sam wondered.

"Oh, small deer, rabbits—you'd be surprised," the lieutenant smiled. "We think it's a good sign. They're obviously running out of food."

"Obviously," Sam grunted.

J.B. stuck his head in a newspaper and remained very still until he heard the door close behind the lieutenant and Pandora.

The others were remarkably courteous to him throughout dinner.

* * *

Pandora came tripping down the steps of the laboratory the following afternoon. J.B. swiveled around slowly, and came face to face with a Coke.

"Is that a peace offering?" he asked, reaching for the can.

Pandora withdrew it. "No, it's not a peace offering. Why would I need one?"

"You'd know that better than I." He swiveled back and concentrated on tapping a command into the computer. She slammed the can down on the console and he flinched.

"You're just being a brat, J.B." She moved around the table to face him, hands on hips, and glared until he looked up. And laughed.

"What are you laughing at?" she demanded. She brushed her hair back with one hand, pulled the top of her shirt together.

"I'm trying not to be a brat . . . and I couldn't help thinking . . . ." He shrugged.

She softened. "Thinking what?"

He shrugged again. "You really are beautiful . . . ."

"Don't. Please." But she came back around the table and put her arm around his shoulders. He reached up for her and they kissed.

"Is this a monogamous relationship or what?" he mumbled.

"It's very monogamous. But I think I'm allowed to keep the hounds off your scent. Really, J.B., I'm sure he'll stop coming around after those cowboys leave. I'm not encouraging him, you know."

"I know."

Another kiss . . . longer.

"Now why don't you relax, and come on over for dinner later?"

"Yes, ma'am."

Chapter 39

He was heading straight for the Washington Club West, and a vigilant Pandora was ready to meet him when he slipped off the roan and slapped at his seat with a leather glove.

It was only then, with the characteristic feminine gesture, that Pandora realized it was a woman.

"Can I help you?" she inquired, in a cool voice that promised anything but help. Leaving the lab, she had watched the puffs of dust resolve themselves into a diagonal trail from the shack of the cactus barons across the plain.

"I'm sure you can, honey. I just came to borrow a cup of sugar."

She laughed as Pandora crossed her arms and inclined her head to one side.

"Actually, I was kinda curious about this place. What in tarnation you folks doin' out here?"

Pandora did not respond except to draw a corner of her mouth down a trifle more.

The woman tugged at her gloved hand and shot it out. "I'm Lilly Mae Spitzberger."

Slowly Pandora extended her arm. "Pandora."

"Mmm. Well, Pandora," Lilly Mae rattled on, "you can understand how we'd be a touch curious, expectin' nothin' but a bunch of potholes out here, where the army's supposed to be testing missiles, or some such, and then findin' this little community of trailers . . . ."

Pandora regarded the short, straight gray hair, the crisp checked shirt beneath the leather vest, the slim hips encased in jeans above those pointy-toed boots that tortured her own feet. She was five-foot-five, but she found herself looking up at the older woman.

"This is a restricted site, ma'am," she enunciated quietly.

"Well, 'course I don't mean to cause you no trouble, Pandora, or embarrass you none," Lilly Mae assured her.

They turned at the creak of the metal door. Sam took in the visitor at one sweep.

"Pandora," he rasped, "aren't you going to invite our guest in?"

He stood to one side, indicating the entry with a tumbler of bourbon and water. Lilly Mae stepped past him, trailing a thank you, as he stared down a surly Pandora.

"Care for something to drink, ma'am? And please, call me Sam."

"Please call me Lilly Mae," said Lilly Mae, who was admiring the leather couches, the thick pile of the carpet. She turned and peered into Sam's glass. "That looks about right."

Pandora slumped into an armchair while Sam went to fetch the drink himself.

"Is he your man, honey?" Lilly Mae asked.

Pandora drew herself up in reproach. Then she laughed. "No, he is not my man."

"Here you go," Sam said, handing Lilly Mae a drink. Pandora coughed. "Sorry, Pandora," Sam apologized, "guess I'm not used to playing gentleman." He and Lilly Mae exchanged smiles.

"You sure got a nice little setup here," the older woman observed. "You folks takin' a sabbatical or somethin'?"

"No, no," Sam protested. "Well . . . actually, I guess you could say we are. I am. And what about you, Lilly Mae? What are you doing in these parts?"

"Lived here most of my life," Lilly Mae declared, as Pandora sank deeper into her chair. She watched them fold themselves into a leather couch, heads together, subdued voices punctuated by a laugh, a giggle, and closed her eyes.

When she opened them, Sam was standing before the picture window, humming, accompanied by the rattling of ice in his glass.

"Where's Lilly Mae?"

He glanced at her and turned back to the window. "Had to go. She's cooking for the guys back at the ranch."

"Did she get her cup of sugar?" Pandora asked.

Sam shook the glass. "What cup of sugar?"

Chapter 40

Sam came striding in, in the middle of dinner, the following evening, followed by a burbling Bob. Pandora tracked the older man as he took his customary chair and lowered his head over the bowl of soup Alfie slipped before him.

"Well. Where have you two been all day?" she asked.

"Just paying a visit to the neighbors," Sam replied. He looked up at her briefly. "Is that all right . . . mother?"

"I got some terrific shots, Pandora," Bob broke in. "Those fellows have great faces."

"They seemed rather seedy to me," Pandora remarked, "except for Lilly Mae, of course."

Morgan perked up. "Who's Lilly Mae?" he asked. Pandora was concentrating on slicing up a tenderloin tip.

Sam appealed for understanding to the men seated around the table. "She's a very nice lady who came out to support the cowboys. She's cooking for the old geezers." He turned to Pandora. "All us boys need a den mother." Pandora ignored him.

Sam sucked at his bottle of beer and hesitated. Then he told them about Lilly Mae. She had been married to a man whose family had, along with about a hundred others, agreed to move off their ranches in the early forties, when the government claimed it needed the land for the war effort. After the war, however, the government insisted it still needed the land, and decided to lease it, making annual payments to the ranchers. That was about the time Lilly Mae Bollinger met Harold Spitzberger. While she continued teaching math and science to the children of oilmen and ranchers and ex-ranchers, he went to school, studying animal husbandry and working part-time in a dry goods store, dreaming of the day when his family would get the ranch back and he would develop a cattle business along modern scientific principles.

But his parents died, the dream dissolved with the years, and Harold grew bitter. In 1970, the government declared that the lease payments it had made over the years constituted sufficient payment for the land. In 1976, the government began condemning the lands and confiscating them. Harold had a heart attack six months later.

"Seventy-six," Pandora repeated.

"Yes," Sam drawled, "the bicentennial of the Declaration of Independence."

Bob looked confused. "Yes . . . but . . . national defense . . . national security was involved."

"National bullshit."

All heads turned toward Sam, who picked up knife and fork and resumed masticating prime beef.

Bob stepped gingerly into the silence. "But those guys all got paid for the land. Isn't that what Jenkins said?"

"It came in dribs and drabs," Sam explained, "not enough at a time to do anything with . . . buy a new place. And they didn't get anything for their grazing rights."

"Grazing rights," Pandora frowned. "Isn't that just the right to graze cattle on federal land?" Sam nodded. "Well, that land didn't belong to them anyway," she argued. "It belonged to the federal government to start with."

"True enough," Morgan offered, "but these little ranches around here aren't worth a dime without their grazing rights."

"Besides," said Sam, "some other ranchers farther south who were bought out later got paid for their grazing rights . . . they were taken into consideration, and the ranchers got a lump sum . . . . The White Sands folks just got strung along."

Pandora studied him. "You seem to have learned quite a bit today," she said.

"And he got another lesson," Bob confided, leaning forward. "In horseback riding."

Sam always looked rumpled. But now they noticed the dust edging the sleeves of his jacket, the smudge on his shirt, the sunburned nose. Pained by the examination, he pushed back his chair and stood. "Think I'll mosey into town tomorrow and get me some boots."

Chapter 41

J.B. rolled over and pulled the pillow over his head, but still he could hear the knocking. "What in blazes . . . ." he began, but Pandora was stepping into her robe and stumbling toward the door.

The sunlight blinded her for a moment, and then she was yawning into the beaming face of Lieutenant Jenkins.

"I guess it is a little early," he laughed, "but it's such a beautiful day. I wanted to get out early. I thought you might like to go for a Sunday drive. We could have breakfast in town. Maybe Las Cruces . . . or Juárez." He was holding his hat in both hands, searching her face.

Pandora stammered, rubbed her head, glanced back toward the bedroom and stammered again.

"Come on," he urged, "we'll have a great time. I'll wait for you in the jeep."

Her "but" slid softly off his back.

"It's only seven-thirty!" J.B. protested. "What in Christ's name . . . . Who the hell does he . . . ."

Pandora dressed quickly to escape his sputtering, trying to soothe him all the while.

"I'll be back before you know it, J.B. It's probably the last time . . . ."

She slammed her hat on her head and closed the door behind her.

* * *

"I didn't realize Mexico was so close," Pandora marveled, as they drove across the bridge spanning the Rio Grande. They moved slowly but steadily in the long line of traffic composed partly of tourists, partly of Mexicans returning home after a week of work in American homes and businesses. No one was interested in what they might be bringing into Mexico, only in what was going out. The opposing line progressed in fits and starts, as U.S. customs agents scoured selected cars and pedestrians.

Even as they neared the end of the bridge, the air seemed to change. Perhaps it was the music blaring from distant shops, or the humidity steaming from the river. Mexico breathed abandon, fiesta, and danger, as if warning that pleasure had its price.

Pandora and the lieutenant parked on a street off the main avenue and strolled past the shops, dodging small boys trying to lure them into dark places.

The scent of baking bread drew them into a pastelería. They bought bollitos, large crusty brown rolls resembling small footballs, and soft floury biscuits. The lieutenant interpreted, in fluent, unmusical Spanish.

They crossed a narrow street in front of a Harley-Davidson. The long-haired driver, from under a cowboy hat, followed Pandora's progression, eyes hidden behind sunglasses. Pandora was reminded of the cowboys camped at the missile range.

"What?"

"I said, there's a nice clean little place just down the street," Lieutenant Jenkins repeated. "I thought we might have breakfast there."

"That's fine," Pandora agreed.

A dozen tables with red-checkered cloths were scattered around the cafe. They chose a booth in front of the window.

The streets were filling with old Fords and Chevys, and an occasional Toyota pickup. Mexican families were emerging from church for their Sunday outing. The Harley-Davidson cruised by.

"You're awfully quiet," Lieutenant Jenkins remarked.

Pandora turned from the window. "I don't get off the base very much. I'm having a good time just people-watching."

"Yes, this is a good place for it. Have you been at the base long?"

"Oh, a couple of months," Pandora replied.

The lieutenant stirred his coffee. "I can't help feeling I've seen that fellow Jim before."

Pandora shrugged. "Maybe you have . . . maybe at another base."

He frowned. "No . . . I don't think so."

Pandora pierced the egg sitting atop her enchilada with a fork, and concentrated on sopping up the yolk with rice.

Outside again, they maneuvered around women in bright print dresses and men in straw hats. They walked down a few blocks, then crossed the street and turned back.

A child of about eight coaxed them into a shop with a smile. They wandered farther and farther into the cavern, darkened by walls hung with hundreds of paintings on black, sometimes red, velvet. Benito Juárez on velvet, Don Quixote on velvet, deer and wolves and owls on velvet, even the Pope on velvet. They admired the technique even while deploring the effect. Skill in the service of kitsch.

The velvet absorbed sound, cast a pall on the ashtrays, bookends, chess sets of onyx. By the time they had rounded the shop, they were eager to escape into the sunlight.

A fluffy pink paper horse caught Pandora's attention two doors down.

"Piñatas," Jenkins pronounced, explaining that the papier-mâché animals were stuffed with candies, and how blindfolded children tried to smash them open with sticks or clubs.

Pandora was offended by the fate of such beautiful creatures. From the rainbow-hued bestiary, she selected a purple burro.

"I'll take care of it," the lieutenant offered.

"No, no, please," Pandora protested.

"It's my pleasure," Jenkins insisted. "Maybe I can help you do it in, to celebrate . . . something," he smiled. She relented.

A block later, he drew her into a liquor store.

"The prices are fantastic. Look at this, Johnnie Walker black for ten dollars."

Pandora nodded, clutching her burro. Glancing down an aisle, she spied bottles of sour mash.

Jenkins' eyebrows rose. "Sour mash?" He pointed out the display of Grand Marnier, bottles of Kahlua among endless rows of tequila. "Wouldn't you prefer one of these?"

Pandora's nose rose, as she turned toward the checkout counter. "No. This is just what I want."

* * *

J.B. was emerging from his own cavern when the jeep drove up. Lieutenant Jenkins nodded, cocked his head. "I don't suppose you've ever been to Cleveland."

"Nope." He helped Pandora out of the jeep, then crossed his arms and stood squarely in front of the driver's door.

"Well," began Lieutenant Jenkins.

"I had a lovely time, Tim," Pandora continued. "Thank you." She reached forward to shake his hand.

"Yes, I certainly did, too . . . . I hope we can do it again."

"Thank you for the piñata."

"My pleasure."

Under the combined weight of Pandora's smile and J.B.'s gaze, Lieutenant Jenkins started the motor. The jeep circled carefully, there was a half salute from the lieutenant, and then both disappeared behind a curtain of dust.

They had hardly taken two steps when another vehicle lurched past them. A smiling Lilly Mae waved from the passenger side. Sam glared resolutely ahead, cigar clamped in his mouth, trying to stay just beyond the roiling dust of the departing jeep.

"Come to White Sands and find romance," J.B. intoned.

"Why not?" Pandora eyed him, slipping her arm through his.

J.B. shrugged. "More power to him, but it's hard to imagine Sam falling for a cowgirl. She just doesn't sound like his type."

"She's hardly a girl . . . but she is very attractive. And I'm not sure 'type' has anything to do with it."

"Nonsense," J.B. argued. "I knew from the first minute I saw you, you were my type."

"Yes," drawled Pandora, "'woman.'"

* * *

Lilly Mae and Sam ate barbecued beef at a small roadhouse on the outskirts of Las Cruces that she had pointed out.

"We used to come here sometimes, Harold and I, just to get away from the White Sands ranchers," she reminisced. "To see people with other kinds of problems, other heartaches."

Sam covered her hand with his. "What would you like to do now?"

Her eyes sparkled and she glanced at the felt-covered tables in an adjoining room. "Let's shoot some pool," she challenged him.

"I'm a little rusty," Sam warned, as a premonition of disaster and disgrace assailed him.

"Oh, don't worry about that," Lilly Mae reassured him, moving between the tables to the other room. "I hardly ever get a chance to play. Teachers are expected to disdain such immoral pastimes, you know. But I love it . . . Harold taught me."

And so, over bourbon and water, she took him apart and put him back together.

"Why, you old hustler," Sam marveled, as she sank the eight-ball with a bank shot for the second time.

"Watch who you're callin' old, old man," she retorted. He smiled as he put another quarter in the slot and racked the balls again.

The pace slowed. Lilly Mae recounted how she had met Harold at a dance in Tularosa she had attended only at the urging of new friends in Roswell. She had arrived in New Mexico from Oklahoma only a few months earlier, and the couple were determined to find a mate for her. She smiled. Harold had been the only man tall enough to chance a waltz with the gangling newcomer.

Sam thought of other dances, other days. He remembered a small, dark-haired woman who floated in his arms, laughing like this woman, teasing, challenging, who made him feel ten feet tall.

"Did you have children?"

"What? Oh. No. We never got around to it."

"We didn't either," said Lilly Mae. "Thought we'd wait until we got the ranch back and settled in . . . ."

"What will you do, Lilly Mae, when the cactus barons leave?"

"Why, keep on doin' what I been doin' all these years . . . teachin' school, and goin' to the Garden Club, tutorin' Mescans so they can get their citizenship . . . ."

Sam's dark brows rose. He sank a striped ball in a corner pocket and straightened. "Your twang is back."

"It comes and goes," Lilly Mae admitted, chalking her cue.

"Yeah," Sam muttered, leaning into the next shot, "it comes and goes."

Chapter 42

J.B. was savoring sour mash when Alfie knocked on the door of Pandora's trailer. There was a phone call for her at Club West.

J.B. pulled off his boots and turned on the TV. Whatever happened to "Your Hit Parade," he wondered, watching the laundered, unlined faces move through a narrow repertoire of expressions in response to some family dilemma. Well, that wasn't so terrific either, but he'd rather listen to any kind of music than the absurd calamities of middle American families, or the absurdly trivial problems of the yuppies.

"That was Tim," Pandora announced. "He says three of the cactus barons rode out yesterday, four more left today."

"It is getting warm out here," J.B. observed. "Not to mention crowded."

She slipped onto the sofa beside him and put her arm through his.

"It'll all be over very soon."

"How'd they get out? Cut the fence again?"

She chuckled. "No. The army put in a temporary gate. And set up a guard post."

He rubbed a finger along her forearm. "So when's your next date?"

"I told him I couldn't make it."

J.B. turned and kissed her loudly. "We'll have to celebrate the passing of the guard. Have a party . . . with your piñata."

Pandora retrieved her arm and glowered at him.

"No one touches my burro."

Chapter 43

A lone rider departed the next day, and by the end of the week, they were all gone. Soon the shack would begin to settle into the earth. The insistent wind would loosen a corner of the roof, small animals would burrow under the walls, wasps would daub their mud nests on the roof beams. The building would join those thousands of other deserted shacks scattered throughout the West, a memory of rains that had stopped coming, of endless grasslands denuded by too many cows, of proprietary fences encroaching on open range. A memory of failure.

Or perhaps a missile from south of State Highway 70 would obliterate the shack, leaving only a small crater.

Lieutenant Timothy Jenkins refused to be consigned to memory. He continued to appear periodically at Club West, chatting with anyone who would talk to him.

Since he displayed little knowledge of poker, photography or politics, Bob and Sam soon withdrew their interest in his visits. Sonny shared his enthusiasm for computer technology, but that subject was as quickly exhausted as that of the symbolism of the Mayan ball court, in which Morgan seemed to have more than a passing interest. As dinner invitations became rarer, he took to knocking on Pandora's door in late afternoon, staying just long enough to watch J.B.'s departure from the lab.

"What does he do in there?" he asked one day, following J.B.'s progress toward his quarters.

"You know I can't say anything about that," Pandora reproved him. "It's a matter of national security."

Jenkins grunted. There was no appeal from that handy little rubber stamp of a phrase.

He turned from the window and brightened. "How about a game of backgammon? Do you have a board? I have a set back at the base I could—."

Pandora sidled in front of a bookcase. "I really never was able to get the hang of that game." She looked at her watch.

"Yes, well, I suppose I'd better be getting back to the base." There was no objection.

"See you again soon," Jenkins smiled, taking Pandora's hands in his.

"Thank you for coming by," she replied.

Chapter 44

Bob had spread the photos on the dining table. More gorgeous sunsets, craggy mountains. J.B. rounded the table and headed for the kitchen. He pulled a Tecate from the refrigerator, twisted off the cap, and sipped.

Amid the "mms" and "ahs" Bob was saying, "I told you they had great faces. And here's a good one of Lilly Mae."

Now his curiosity was piqued, for, except for a hand waving from a wagon and a blur of gray hair, he had never seen the woman who had softened Sam's growl.

He had to peer over the shoulder of Sam, who had picked up the photo and was appraising it, chomping rhythmically on his cigar.

"Damn good-looking woman," J.B. commented. Sam gave a final chomp. "Not bad," he said.

"You ought to invite her over here sometime," Bob suggested.

"I don't believe she has a security clearance," Sam responded. "This isn't exactly a social club, you know."

"Sounds like trouble in paradise," J.B. remarked.

Sam shrugged. "We had a fight."

"A fight?"

Sam was chomping again. "Stubbornest woman I ever met. She thinks the U.S. government is the enemy, and everyone associated with it is either a fool or a crook."

"What category did she put you in?" J.B. smiled.

"It's not funny," Sam reproved him. "I've spent my life in politics. I love politics. Sure it's a game, but it's a game I'm good at. It's not just power—it's the function of power . . . whether it'll be used to line the fat cats' pockets, or help decent people live decent lives." He looked down at the photo in his hand. "Lilly Mae thinks people ought to be left alone to work things out themselves—even if they can't work things out, because they're too dumb, or too black, or too poor."

J.B. sipped his beer. "Lilly Mae hasn't had the best of experiences with the federal government," he noted.

"Damn military and all their parasites," Sam muttered, "arrogant bastards and incompetent bureaucrats. Well, nothing's perfect. But even Lilly Mae's all in favor of bigger and better bombs—as long as they build them on someone else's property."

He placed the photo on the table with a snap.

J.B. followed his gesture and glanced at the other shots.

"This one is Jack Hackleberry," Bob pointed out for J.B., "the old-timer who was trying to reclaim his land."

J.B. nodded, taking in the proud, disintegrating face, the claw gripping the barrel of the shotgun. He moved on to a shot of Sam struggling to mount a roan, then one of him sitting gingerly astride it. The faces of the old men drew him. Great faces, yes, for a camera. But to J.B. they looked defeated rather than strong, in spite of the occasional smile, beaten by life as well as weather. The group photos reminded him of snapshots in a tattered album, of ancestors long gone. His gaze moved on, snapped back. He was conscious of the icy bottle in his hand.

"Who is this?" he demanded.

Bob looked up and came to stand beside him, and followed his pointing finger. A younger man was hurrying around the side of the shack. "Why, that's Jimmy Joe . . . no, Billy Bob . . . something or other." J.B. stared at the long hair, the barrel chest. Bob looked at him quizzically. "We met him at that bar near Alamogordo . . . Sonny and I . . . that day Sonny was late . . . ."

Pandora. Where was Pandora? But then she was at his side. She studied the figure in the photo, listening to his whispered explanation.

Billy Bob, hell. It was Wild Bill Everett, his erstwhile companion at the state pen, the motorcycle maniac who liked to rape women. Wild Bill skulking around the shack of the cactus barons.

Now he remembered the drunken longhair in the cowboy hat who had tried to run Carl off the road from Los Alamos. Was that Wild Bill, too?

What was he doing slinking around the fringes of their encampment in the desert? Did he know about Straight Arrow, of his, J.B.'s, part in it?

And what did that mean for him? Why wasn't he long gone from New Mexico?

J.B. no longer had the stomach for dinner at the club, or anywhere else. He retreated toward the door.

"Hey, J.B.," Bob called. "What did you think of the pics?"

"Great faces," J.B. pronounced, over his shoulder. Just great.

★   ★   ★

Pandora left early the next morning, after persuading Bob to relinquish the photo of Wild Bill Everett. She made the rounds of bars and motels up and down the Tularosa Valley. Some people thought they recognized the face; none remembered his name or knew where he had come from.

The old men sipping beer at the bar near Alamogordo smirked and snickered when Pandora came through the swinging doors. They had put one over on all she represented. They were not about to divulge any information about one of their own—even if he had been one of their own for only a few days.

"He said he'd help," one of them asserted, "and he helped."

The bartender remembered the man with the strange gray eyes—he had caught him out back forcing the waitress up against an old truck, and taken a swing at him before he ran off. That was just before the roundup. He had appeared only a few days before that, and hadn't been back since.

Pandora reported all to J.B.

"That scum. Why is he dogging me?" J.B. worried.

"Maybe he's not," Pandora suggested. "Maybe he's interested in what's going on here."

"He wouldn't know a laser . . . if it punched a hole in his fat gut."

Pandora winced. "Maybe he's being tutored."

"He's not exactly the spy type."

"Who is?"

Chapter 45

On the morning of August twenty-second, forty-two days after the laser had been put back in operation, they began hauling it up. Again J.B. had measured its progress: a nice round four hundred and fifty miles.

Once more Carl came in to shepherd it to Los Alamos.

He had also brought Bob some filters for his camera. Waiting for breakfast the next morning, Bob examined them, explained their various effects to J.B., and then packed them carefully in a pocket of the camera case.

"I'm going to try them out this morning," he declared, as grave as the commanders must have been who sent missiles flying over the White Sands range.

J.B. cocked his head at Pandora. "Mind if I go for a walk with old Bob here?"

"Of course not," Pandora replied, surprised at his reverting to the role of inmate.

"Why don't you come along, too?" he asked.

She looked dubiously at Bob, then shrugged. "Sure. Maybe we can pack a lunch and have a picnic."

"Great!" Bob agreed. "That sounds terrific."

Alfie shook his head as he stuffed a basket with foil-wrapped packages and a couple of canteens of water.

"You'll fry your brains out there."

"You're just jealous," J.B. accused him. "And how about a couple of bottles of beer?" Alfie complied.

J.B. picked up the basket and almost dropped it. "What'd you put in here, a bomb?"

Alfie smiled sweetly. "Have fun, kids."

Bob led off briskly. Pandora half skipped to keep up with him, trying to hear his chatter about the light, the filters, the features of White Sands. J.B. slogged behind, hampered by the hamper. Occasionally Pandora looked over her shoulder and smiled. J.B. stuck his tongue out at her.

"Up there is Trinity," Bob was saying. "Where they exploded the first A-bomb. They let the folks in to see the site once a year. Personally, I'd just as soon not get too close."

"The radiation has dissipated by now. There's no danger," Pandora assured him.

"That's what they say," Bob said, unconvinced. He looked sideways at her, then away, suddenly aware of her as the possessor of arcane knowledge.

"I'd rather shoot these mountains, anyway," he added, squaring his fingers to enclose a peak to the east.

J.B. took advantage of the stop to drop the basket. He slumped down beside it.

"Let's take a rest," he called out. There was no response, and he jumped up and grabbed the basket when they moved on.

He balked when Bob climbed a low hill, helping Pandora up through the grass, and waited below while Bob turned his camera to the western hills. When they disappeared over the top, he stumbled around the base, to where another hill lifted out of the desert floor, and then another. Winding his way through the lowlands, he emerged eventually onto level ground. They were a hundred feet ahead of him.

Groaning and perspiring, he took a diagonal path to a dark spur of volcanic rock, and dropped down, panting.

"I don't think I can go much farther," he shouted. Bob and Pandora turned to look at him curiously, and Bob, apparently more intrigued by the rock than by J.B., began moving his way, snapping every few feet.

"Say," he called, "why don't we have a little snack now—to keep up our strength?"

Bob stopped. "It's only eleven," he complained. "I've hardly had time to try out one filter."

"It's healthier to eat a lot of little meals, instead of one big one," J.B. persisted. "Anyway, I need a drink of water." He proceeded to open the basket, arousing Pandora's curiosity.

"Pickles. Hot peppers, sweet peppers. Olives. Look at all these jars. No wonder the damn thing weighs a ton."

"He was trying to discourage you, I guess," Pandora suggested, unwrapping a sandwich.

"He's doing a terrific job." J.B. leaned over. "What's that?"

Pandora bit into the sandwich. "Ham and swiss."

"Not very imaginative," J.B. sniffed. "Alfie's slipping."

"How about a taco with everything?" She offered him the half-opened package.

"Now that's more like it."

Pandora slipped down beside him at the base of the rock and they munched hungrily. Bob hesitated, then stomped over.

"OK, OK, if you insist." He discarded two packages before he found roast beef, and sat down a little apart from them, next to a dead cholla.

"Not much shade out here," he said, looking around as he took the camera and case from around his neck.

"We're not supposed to be out here in the middle of the day," Pandora pointed out. "Even animals know enough to stay out of the sun."

"Wonder where they go," Bob murmured, biting into his roast beef.

"Oh, they probably burrow under one of these rocks," J.B. surmised.

Bob, who had been about to lean back against the boulder, sat up straight.

"It's awfully menacing, isn't it—the desert, I mean—in a quiet sort of way."

"It depends on what's in your head," said J.B., fishing for a beer. "Say, look at this." He held up a red-checked tablecloth. "I almost missed it."

"Alfie outdid himself," said Pandora, helping him spread the cloth.

"I don't suppose there's an umbrella in there," Bob lamented, "and maybe a couple of chairs." He moved one haunch, then the other. "This grass is kind of scratchy."

"No," said J.B., rummaging through the basket, "don't think so."

He found another taco, poured hot sauce on it, and leaned back, studying the distant smoky blue hills and the gray outcroppings of rock in front of them that lined the desert plain on the west. "What are these mountains, anyway?"

Bob pulled out a map. "Those are the Sierra Caballo—I think."

"Cah-by-yo," J.B. corrected him, nodding now as he scanned the horizon. He was remembering the maps he had seen in the library at the penitentiary. "Yeah, I think you were right about this desert, Bob. If I'm not mistaken, we're in the Jornada del Muerto."

139

"What's that?"

"Dead man's march." Bob choked on his roast beef, and looked warily around him, as if expecting to see a skeleton. "After the first few times the Spaniards came up here from Mexico," J.B. continued, "they started coming through here, to avoid the Apaches. If they walked up along the Rio Grande, the Indians would come down from the mountain passes and surprise them. This route was the lesser of two evils—about a hundred miles long, with no water."

Now Bob scrutinized the Caballos, on the alert for Indians.

"Yep," said J.B., "it's the perfect place for a missile range." He turned to Pandora. "By the way, isn't it a little dangerous for us to be camped in the middle of a missile range?"

"They won't be using this area for a while. They're working on longer-range missiles." J.B. watched her tilt up a canteen and take a swallow. When he turned back, there was a dirty argyle sock draped under the far side of the cholla.

"What's the matter?" Bob asked him, leaning forward slightly. The sock moved.

As quietly and deliberately as he could, J.B. spoke. "Bob. Stay absolutely still. Just—don't move. There's a rattlesnake behind you."

Bob flinched but caught himself. "If you don't move, it won't hurt you . . . probably just slither away." Bob shut his eyes, then opened them. J.B. was still staring behind him. Pandora clutched her stomach.

J.B. moved his head very slowly to one side. A rock. A stick. Anything. There was nothing. How long could they sit immobile? Sweat streamed down Bob's face. Out of the corner of his eye, J.B. saw Pandora's arm move, slowly, as if she were sleepwalking.

She brought her other arm up. The gun looked incredibly small. Where in hell has she been hiding that, he wondered with awe.

"Bob," she said, very calm and low, "when I fire, dive over here. On three. One . . . two . . . ."

"Three" coincided with the pfft of a shot fired with a silencer. It took Bob a second to realize the gun had fired, and then he threw himself across the tablecloth, knocking over jars of pickles and peppers. Pandora fired again and missed. But the first shot had struck the rattler in the head. They watched it coil and uncoil for twenty minutes. Then the reflex died.

J.B. turned at the clink of metal on metal, as Pandora replaced the gun behind the big silver belt buckle.

Bob had scrambled to his feet and was staring alternately at the snake and Pandora.

"Well," he breathed, "I've had it for today. You guys ready to go back?"

"You go on," J.B. said, "Pandora and I are going to do a little scouting." He ignored her frown.

"OK," said Bob, gathering his camera and equipment. "See you back at the ranch." He hesitated, eyeing Pandora, before turning. "Be careful," he called back.

J.B. was packing up the picnic paraphernalia.

"What's this scouting business?" she asked.

"Oh, I just want to get a look at those rocks over there," he explained, emptying the jars and kicking dirt over the contents. She made a face. "Don't worry, it'll probably get composted by a missile one of these days."

He swung the basket up onto his shoulder and took her hand.

"J.B., those mountains are miles away."

"We'll take it slow. Watch out for rattlesnakes and things." She said nothing and let him lead her toward the San Andres.

Half an hour later, they were climbing into the rocky foothills. She glanced back over her shoulder. There was no sign of their passing, no indication that any human had traversed that grassy basin humped by solitary hills and frozen flows of lava.

"J.B., we're going to get lost."

"Hey, what happened to your Mata Hari training? Haven't you heard of celestial navigation?"

"Yes. I also learned how to change a tire, but I've never had to do it."

"Stop bragging. But you do have good legs." He whirled her out in front of him, running his eyes over her, and she laughed. "Even if you don't show them very much." He wrinkled his nose at her pants.

"It's too hot to go running around out here in a bikini. You know, a person could die out here—of exposure."

"You have to expose something first," he replied, examining the terrain ahead of them. "Let's go this way."

"Why?" she groaned. "What's the difference? It's all the same."

"I know," he commiserated, "you've seen one rock, you've seen them all."

She followed him up a spur and broke from his grasp. "I have to rest," she gasped, and sank down. A stand of grass molded itself around her, and she rocked in it.

"J.B.," she said gravely, "I think we're really lost. And I have a ton of dirt in my boots." She grabbed at one, but he backed up to her and took it between his legs.

"Push," he ordered.

She raised her eyebrows. "Let's see," she said, "is this the way they do it in the movies?" She set her other foot against his rump and pushed. He landed on the ground, the boot in his hands.

"Christ Almighty, woman, gently!"

Pandora giggled. "Yes, sir. I mean, yes, suh, Colonel Bowie." She saluted, and he scurried toward her like a crab.

"Hold on, now, J.B.," she warned, trying to back away, but he grabbed her foot and pulled her down flat. He hung over her, staring into her face. "J.B.," she whispered, "not here."

He paused. Then sat back and tore her sock off. "How about here?" he asked, raising her foot and kissing the sole. He let her go and grinned.

Pandora sighed. "Disappointed?" he asked.

"Damn you, J.B.!" she shouted, and lunged for him, but he was up and away, slithering down the other side of the boulder, laughing at the sky.

"Wait!" Pandora yelled, "don't leave me!" She reached for the boot and the sock and tugged them on, and stumbled after him, muttering. He slowed his pace to let her catch up.

Twisting through the jumble of boulders, finding footholds in the shadowed crevices between them, they climbed higher. A patch of yellow alyssum sang out among the bare rocks. From a cleft, a stunted arm of juniper reached out. A path opened before them and they followed it downward. Then the rocks parted and they came out into a small basin rimmed by peaks. From the top of a lone pinnacle of rock, a raven hiccupped.

"J.B., I'm dying of thirst," Pandora said. "Is there any water left?" She peered up at the clouds gathering above the peaks.

"Have a swig."

She took a long pull from the canteen and handed it back. J.B. put the cap on and tossed it into the basket. "Feeling better?"

"Much."

"We'll just rest for a few minutes and go on back."

"Good idea," Pandora said. "The Garden of Eden, it's not." She turned in a half-circle and stopped. "Look at that."

He followed her outstretched arm. An odd finger of rock poked out from a cluster of boulders. "Let's go see," he said, taking her hand.

When they neared the boulders, they could see that the outcrop was not rock, but a ragged piece of timber. J.B. brushed dirt away, uncovering part of another beam. "Come on, let's see what's under here."

They brushed and scraped the dirt and stones away with their hands, slowly, cursing when a splinter of wood caught them. J.B. gave Pandora a handkerchief to wrap around one hand. By the time they had exposed the shaft, it was in tatters.

"Is it a mine?" Pandora whispered, as J.B. tore the last of the rotting wood away.

"Seems someone just boarded up an old cave." J.B. crouched and stepped through the low entrance. After a few feet, the ceiling rose and the walls sloped back. It was cool and pleasant after the desert sun.

"Come on in," he called.

Pandora ducked and stepped inside. "Probably a million creepy-crawlies in here," she complained.

"If there are, they're probably dead. Where's your spirit of adventure?" he challenged, moving ahead.

Pandora grabbed his shirt and he started. "Don't do that," he said.

"Don't you do that," she retorted. "I don't want to lose you."

"You mean you don't want to get lost," J.B. corrected her, laughing. He took her hand and they walked on, wrapped in a shaft of gold from the late afternoon sun that blazed a path for some twenty feet. The ground sloped downward, then leveled out. The walls drew back into the pulsing darkness. No, it was his breathing, and the pulse he felt in Pandora's wrist. He released it and took his shirt off and spread it on the ground. He pulled her down with him.

"Now, what were you saying about not wanting to lose me?"

"J.B., this place is spooky. Aren't you afraid of snakes and—."

He stopped her with his mouth. Her arms went up around his neck and she lay back.

She looked up once, as a last finger of flame tried to hold off the enveloping purple sky. He licked the reflected glow off her chin as she bent down to him.

* * *

Hours later she stirred and rolled over. She threw out an arm, and instantly she was awake, blinking. She reached for J.B. and felt only cold rock. "J.B.! For God's sake, get up, J.B."

She crawled a few feet and swept the floor with her hand. Now she was disoriented. "J.B.!" she hissed. She sat back on her haunches and struck her head on a protruding rock. She wailed.

"What's the matter?" J.B. mumbled. "Pandora? Where are you?"

"Here. Wherever that is."

J.B. rummaged through their clothes. "Just a minute . . . hold on. I got it." His cigarette lighter flared. "Holy Jesus."

"What is it?" she whispered, starting toward him.

The light went out and he flicked the lighter twice. "Damn. Turn around. Look behind you."

"J.B.," she began, but she relaxed as he came toward her. He held the lighter up near her head and she turned.

She had hit her head on what appeared to be a black brick, one of dozens, or hundreds, that lined the wall of the cave. He moved the lighter slowly, revealing more bricks piled in the center of the cave and along the opposite wall.

"So?" Pandora asked.

"Well, just wait. Here, hold the lighter." He searched the floor of the cave with his hands, grumbling when Pandora let the light go out. "Here we are," he said, turning back with a small flat rock. Fumbling with one of the bricks, he finally dislodged it. He cradled it in his lap and began scraping with the rock. A shine of yellow appeared.

"That's not what I think it is—is it?" Pandora asked.

J.B. was chortling. "Shacked up in a bed of gold. And you thought it was spooky."

"It is," Pandora insisted. "Where did it come from?"

He ran his hand over the bars. "Can't make out any markings. But I'll bet it's the treasure of Victorio." He sat back looking pleased with himself.

"What's that?" Pandora asked. "Looks like your ordinary bank robbery to me."

"Not so ordinary, my love." The light died as J.B. swung around to sit beside her. "No, save it," he admonished as she tried to rekindle the flame. "Sometime in the thirties, an old codger stumbled into a cave around here, and supposedly found a horde of gold bars. He took some of them out, and hid them in various caches. This could be the main cave, or one of his hiding places. Anyway, he was later killed by one of his partners. Others tried and failed to find the treasure. When the army took over White Sands in the forties, no one was allowed to come looking for it. Someone tried, just a few years ago. It was a big story up in Santa Fe."

"But who put it here, in the first place?"

"Well, it could have been stolen by Victorio and his Apaches from Wells Fargo shipments. But there's another legend, that a Spanish priest found a rich vein of gold, manufactured the bars with his Indian followers, and hid them here . . . to keep the Mexican authorities from confiscating them."

"And we've found them."

"You found them." He groped for her head. "How do you feel?"

"Dizzy. But not from the bump . . . . I suppose we should report this . . . to the authorities."

"What authorities?" J.B. blurted. "The army? They'd just use it to build bigger and better weapons."

He was silent. The ghosts of Victorio and the Spanish priest and all the treasure-hunters who had poked their noses into the San Andres Mountains seemed to press closer. He felt Pandora shiver.

"Do you realize what this means, Pandora?" he asked finally. "We have an out."

There was a pause. "What do you mean?"

"We don't have to sweat for them anymore. Just a few of these bars would take care of us for the rest of our lives. We could go to South America—."

She laughed. "Like a million other people have tried to do."

"Well, that's just for a start," he protested. "Once we cash some of these in, we can go anywhere. Get any kind of passports we want. How'd you like to go to Marrakesh . . . or Samarkand?"

She laughed again, low in her throat. "What would we do, J.B.?"

"We wouldn't have to do anything. You could take care of the kids, and I'd stroll over to the bazaar every morning for a cup of coffee and the newspaper." He was enjoying the vision. "You could dress in those filmy things," he continued, "while I took care of investments and other business."

"Male chauvinist!"

"Well, then I'd take care of the kids, and you could handle the finances."

The silence bounced off the black bricks and thudded in their ears. What was he saying, J.B. wondered. What was she thinking? What were the limits of possibility? The ghosts of Victorio and the Spanish priest smiled and withdrew.

"How would we ever get it out of here?" she asked in a small voice.

"I don't know . . . . We'd need a plan."

There was a click and Pandora stared at him over the cigarette lighter. For the first time, he felt naked.

"You're right," he said brusquely, rising, "let's go."

They dressed quickly and silently. J.B. took a last look around the treasure room, then hefted the telltale brick in his hands. He placed it in the picnic basket. "Just a little souvenir," he explained.

"Is it heavy?"

"About fifty pounds worth. Go ahead, you lead."

They emerged, blinking, into the morning sun. J.B. set the basket down to replace the timbers and heap dirt over them. Then they set off.

The wind was up, but above it they could hear a mechanical whining. They looked up to see a small plane cruising almost above them.

"Funny," mused Pandora, "this place is off-limits to private planes." And as if it had been awaiting her pronouncement, an army plane suddenly appeared, heading straight for the Cessna. Like a mother hen, it worried the small plane, forcing it to turn eastward toward the boundary of the missile range. The Cessna flew off, followed by the army plane. But not before J.B. had glimpsed a disturbingly familiar face in the co-pilot's seat.

"What is it?" Pandora wanted to know.

He continued staring at the sky.

"J.B."

He turned to her. "It looked like . . . Wild Bill Everett."

He glanced down at the picnic basket, shook his head. "I don't understand. First he's with the ranchers, now here. He's after me for some reason."

She laid her hand gently on his arm. "It must have something to do with Straight Arrow. How could he have known you were here?"

"I don't know . . . but I'm sure he knows now."

"I'll see if I can find out anything when we get back."

He slung the basket up onto one shoulder and started down the mountain. They moved silently for a time, J.B. apparently oblivious to her slipping and stumbling behind, until Pandora could no longer bear his solitary gloom.

"I don't think you can make it all the way to South America today," she taunted, as he stopped to shift the basket to the other shoulder. "Why don't we stop over at beautiful downtown White Sands?"

He grinned as he lumbered up a rock and skidded down the other side, letting the thought of the gold nudge Wild Bill out of his mind. Later, when she took his arm, as if to steady or support him, he felt elated. Maybe he had hold of something here—besides a fifty-pound fantasy.

It was noon when they approached the group of trailers, with no one in sight. They stumbled forward to J.B.'s trailer. But once inside, he stared around him in consternation. Where was he to hide the bar, under the mattress? Behind the sofa? And what if, for some reason, they searched his quarters?

Setting down the basket, he wrinkled his brow. "Maybe I should hide it in the lab."

"Sonny or Morgan might find it," Pandora said.

"You're right." He felt desperate. And God, he needed to take a leak. He scowled at the basket.

"That's it!" he shouted, hoisting it and heading for the john. Puzzled, Pandora followed him. He took the lid off the toilet tank and placed it on the floor. Then, gently, he chunked the brick down into the tank. He smiled at Pandora as he replaced the lid. "And just imagine, I'll be conserving water, too."

She tilted her head and rolled her eyes at him.

"Now out, out," he waved her away, "I have some business to attend to."

Chapter 46

J.B. rose early the next morning. There was something special about today, but what was it? Ah, yes, they were scheduled to put the laser down the hole again.

It was only when he entered the bathroom that he remembered the gold. Quickly he lifted the cover from the toilet tank. The bar lay like a lump of coal, only a tiny patch revealing itself.

He replaced the lid, completed the morning ritual of showering, dressing and eating, and marched over to the lab.

Before, J.B. had taken pleasure in watching the cables snake down the hole. Now he was impatient. There were too many other things he wanted to think about. Gold. Mexico. Pandora. Desert isles. Why was it always a desert isle, he wondered, that men dreamed of as a refuge? Desert: barren, dry. Better scratch desert.

And, of course, he was disturbed by the reappearance in his life of Wild Bill Everett. Maybe it was Straight Arrow that he was after.... Did it matter?

He drummed his fingers on the table. He stood up and stretched and thrust his hands in his pockets. The hours stumbled by like drunken sailors.

He switched places with Sonny. It was less frustrating to pay out the cables, monotonous as the work was, than to sit idly at the computer, straightening the hose or a wire now and then. Still, his mind wandered.

"J.B.!" Morgan yelled. "Slow down! You're letting it out too fast."

"Oh. Sorry."

It was three in the morning when they finished. J.B. turned on the laser and dragged himself to bed.

* * *

Pandora had found the private airfield at which a man calling himself Billy Bob Sawyer, along with a tall, thin friend, had rented the Cessna. They had paid good cash money, according to the operator, and he had asked few questions. Once again, she told J.B., there was no trace of Everett.

Now they were more than lovers. They were conspirators. But J.B. sensed a hesitation, a little extra step, between the visions he painted and Pandora's acceptance of them. Come on, woman, let yourself go, take a chance with me, he pleaded silently, trying to coax her mentally into abandoning her reservations and joining him wholeheartedly in planning their escape.

He rhapsodized about Tahiti, enumerated the joys of Pago Pago, adumbrated the beauties of Sri Lanka.

"Do you know that in Sri Lanka, you can find rubies just—."

"Who needs rubies?" Pandora pointed out. "We already have gold."

"Well, of course," he huffed. "I just thought one might look charming in your navel." He lunged at her, but she slipped out from under him, laughing.

"But seriously, J.B., how do we get the gold out . . . and how do we get out of the country?"

"Well, we could hide it under some bales of straw in a wagon, and then ford the Rio Grande. I mean, if Mexicans can get in, why can't we get out? Or maybe a submarine would be . . . ."

Pandora put her arms around him and planted a loud kiss on his cheek. He stared straight ahead.

"How the hell do I know how we get it out?" he mourned. "But if I solved our laser problems, why not this?" He looked unconvinced.

"What about the laser?" she asked. "Are you going to finish the work?"

J.B. hunkered down against the cushions. "Of course not," he muttered. "I mean, sooner or later, something . . . untoward is bound to happen, anyway."

"Untoward?"

"A catastrophe, a disaster!" J.B. exploded, jumping up and stomping around the room. "It's amazing we've gotten this far."

"But—you seemed so confident," she protested.

He whirled. "Did you think I wanted to go back to the pen?" She looked down.

"And there was a chance it would go," he explained, "there still is. It's just that I don't see how our luck can hold out. And I told them," he shook his finger at her, "everything would have to work perfectly, there couldn't be any snags, or it'd be impossible."

Pandora nodded. He watched her snare a red hair on her pants leg, meticulously, between thumb and forefinger, and release it into the ashtray. She looked up to see him staring at her. What was in this woman's mind, he thought. Was she capable of running off with him and a few million dollars, or of turning him in? Could he trust her? What choice did he have?

"J.B.," she said, seemingly in reply, "it's a beautiful idea, running away with all this gold. But like your laser, everything will have to work perfectly."

He bobbed his head. How the hell did he manage to get himself into all these perfectly hopeless situations?

Chapter 47

It was amazing how what appeared to be a means of deliverance, a reason for exultation, could turn so easily into a foretaste of doom, the feeling that no matter what blessings were bestowed on them, what joy they could create for themselves, they were imprisoned in the Dead Man's March of New Mexico and whatever life the U.S. government chose for them after that. J.B. vacillated wildly between dejection and despair.

Through the last days of August and early September they watched the clouds mound in the west, crowding out the intense blue of the sky. They came in silent phalanxes over the desert. In the distance they could see fingers of rain, always reaching toward the earth, never touching it. Never a release.

* * *

"Shit," J.B. spat out. "We're sitting on a fortune, and all we can do is immerse ourselves in gloom."

He was pacing the living room of her trailer, which meant he was growing dizzy from the frequent changes in direction. He sat down.

"Now, what's the problem? The problem is, how to move a caveful of gold bars out from under the nose of the army, to a safe place."

Pandora, curled up on the sofa, watched him expectantly.

"All we've got to do is stay calm and be rational. There's got to be a way, and we can find it." He lit a cigarette and exhaled loudly.

"We've gotten ourselves in a panic," he continued, leaning toward her, "and for what? We just got carried away by the gold."

Pandora gripped her toes and nodded.

"We've got all the time in the world to come up with a solution. Well, a year and a half, at least."

"You're right," she agreed. "I guess it was just the sight of all those gold bars sitting there. I can understand now how people have gone crazy because of gold."

Maybe it was the whisper of fall in the breeze that wafted through the window, a chill breath that promised an end to the stultifying heat of summer. They sat silently for some time, soothed by the coolness.

Pandora brightened. "Maybe *I* could bring them out, one brick at a time. At least, some of them. No one would question my comings and goings."

He shook his head. "Too heavy for you."

Her eyebrows rose. "I could get a shopping cart from Safeway." They both laughed.

"We need a way to get in and out quickly. Load up before anyone knows what's happened and then take off." She blinked under his steady gaze. "Can't you use your—contacts, to get a plane in here?"

"I'm not agent double-0-seven," she objected. "I can't just commandeer an airplane. And anyway, that would certainly attract attention. You saw how quickly that army plane arrived to chase the Cessna away."

"Sometimes I think you don't have the proper spirit of cooperation." He said it lightly, but he was probing.

"That's not true," she flared. "I want this to work as much as you."

He came and sat beside her and ran a finger up above her knee. "Maybe we should discuss this in bed. I think much better when I'm lying down." She moved his hand away, pouting.

He leaned over to kiss her and she turned her cheek to him. He kissed and licked his way over to her lips. By the time he arrived, she had started unbuckling his belt.

Chapter 48

He had been measuring the progress of Straight Arrow, and now he was staring at the configuration on the video screen.

Something was very wrong.

Not with Straight Arrow itself. The vacuum cleaner had sucked its way through some six hundred miles of earth in a little over four months. J.B. felt vindicated, redeemed, by its performance. He might be a convict on the run, but he had answered his country's call in its hour of need (here he imagined an unctuous Arthur with his right hand covering his golden lapel), he had designed a souped-up laser of peculiar proportions but obvious competence, and now he was mothering it on its journey.

But to what end?

To Iran?

Or to Kalamazoo, as Pandora had once suggested.

For the "X" on the screen before him that indicated the position of Straight Arrow had wandered over the boundary of the magic circle.

When had he last checked the direction of the laser? Or done more than glance at the oscilloscope? He swiveled around to study the two peaks on the screen in relation to the grease-pencil flourish with which he had encircled them. The pattern had shifted almost three-sixteenths of an inch to the right. An inconsequential difference at this end, but that fraction would grow and multiply as the distance increased. Eventually, Straight Arrow would be hundreds, perhaps thousands, of feet off course.

Where was it now, he wondered. He had no idea how long the laser had been veering from its course.

Or why.

* * *

"An accident?" repeated Jake Hagstrom. "Not likely."

The Los Alamos programmer had been reviewing the steps he had taken to program the laser in the spring, shaping and smoothing his beard with one hand as he compared the instructions that were now lodged in the computer with the notes he had made initially.

He gave a final tug on the beard. "Here it is."

The notation in the upper left-hand corner of the screen meant nothing to J.B. or Pandora, who stared blankly at the letters and figures.

"It's an entry telling the laser to shift right."

"You didn't put it there . . . by accident?" J.B. ventured.

"Hell, no," Jake responded. "Someone had to do this deliberately."

J.B. and Pandora leaned back, exchanging glances.

"I don't suppose you can tell how long that—entry—has been in there," J.B. said.

Jake shook his head. "No way. Could have been entered anytime after I programmed her." He hesitated and looked up at J.B.

"I can program it to shift left to the same degree; or I can simply erase the entry, and you can start fresh . . . back it up to the point where it went off course. It's up to you."

J.B. turned and walked toward the stairway, regarding his shoes. It was tempting to let the laser continue, instead of having it blast a second path through God knew how many miles of rock. But then he remembered the pipeline that would have to be sent down the hole after the laser had completed its work. He pictured the rigid lengths of pipe trying to snake through the curving tunnel. He sighed and turned back to them.

"We'd better start from scratch. Take it out."

Jake complied with a few taps on the keyboard.

He rose, collecting his notes. "We didn't talk about a secure system . . . just made it simple."

"For the dummy," J.B. grimaced.

Jake laughed. "Well, I added a few tricks to make it more difficult next time." He clapped a hand on J.B.'s shoulder. "But it's pretty hard to keep someone out if he's determined to get in."

After he had left, J.B. and Pandora hurried to Club West. She made two phone calls, one to Arthur, leaving a message for the absent defense secretary to return her call.

"What did your friends have to say?"

"They investigated everyone thoroughly before they came on base. Everyone here was cleared."

"Then it had to be someone from that rancher crowd," J.B. concluded. "Unless your pal Jenkins is a mole," he taunted.

Pandora shook a finger in his face. "Wild Bill. He's the logical one. I told them about his being in the area, when you saw him in the photo, and in the plane, but they haven't gotten a line on him."

J.B. turned and headed for the kitchen to find a beer. "He's not that subtle," he called. "Wild Bill would be more likely to ride a cycle over a computer than to sabotage it."

She was sitting on a couch with her hands folded in her lap when he returned.

"I feel terrible, J.B. It's all my fault."

J.B. sat down beside her. "That's nonsense. You heard what Jake said.... If it's anybody's fault, it was mine. I should have been paying more attention."

He took a sip of beer and pondered. "You know ... actually, I can't figure out why they—somebody—did it. We were bound to discover it sooner or later and make a correction."

"Maybe they just wanted to delay the project," Pandora offered.

"I think it was dumb."

Pandora studied him for a moment. "Maybe they wanted to make you—or Straight Arrow—look dumb."

★ ★ ★

"I don't understand it, either, Mr. President," Arthur commiserated. "Why didn't they just—blow it up?" he asked no one in particular.

The president thumped a pen on his desk. "Are you quite sure this man knows what he's doing?"

"Of course, Mr. President," the secretary of energy, feeling responsible for the project, hastened to assure him.

"He's a very capable man," Arthur added.

The president lifted an eyebrow in Arthur's direction. "I thought you favored some more dynamic action—an invasion, perhaps, or some little adventure like the one the CIA was working up—before we settled on the laser."

"I did, I did," Arthur admitted. "But this is such a delicious way to take revenge on that benighted country."

"Then you think we should continue?"

"Certainly, Mr. President," said Arthur.

Chapter 49

"We have got to get away from here, Pandora."

"We'll find a way. I know you'll think of something, J.B."

He raised his hand. "No, no, I don't mean that. I mean right now. Take a break from Straight Arrow. It's like being in prison again, confined to quarters."

He turned from the sink where he was washing dishes. "How can you stand it out here? I have some semblance of work, but you don't even have that."

"I have some entertainment now and then," she replied, looking him up and down.

He sat down across the table from her. "Isn't there any way we can get out of here for a day or two? See some new faces? Some trees? Christ, I'd settle for a movie."

She pursed her lips. "I don't know whether they'd go for that . . . though you've been such a good boy."

He gave her his most ingratiating smile. "Everyone gets time off for good behavior."

"I'll find out about it."

* * *

Sam poked at a lamb chop. "What's an Oktoberfest?"

"It's a festival they have every year at Cloudcroft," Pandora explained. "They have arts and crafts booths, and you get a tour of the aspens, and lots of beer and sausage."

"Where's Cloudcroft?" Bob asked.

"It's a little town near Alamogordo, up in the mountains, maybe sixty miles from here. It's up in skiing country."

"They ski out here?" Bob was incredulous.

"Of course," Pandora assured him, knowledgeable after a reading of the Chamber of Commerce brochures. "It isn't all desert. In fact, there's a great variety of land forms and life zones in New Mexico."

J.B. dipped his head toward her, admiringly.

"Well, sounds great," said Bob. "I'm kind of tired of cactus, myself."

Sam was suspicious. "Sounds awfully German. Where'd they get a name like that for a festival?"

"Actually," Pandora informed him, "they have a sizable German population around Alamogordo. And they attract quite a few Germans from the missile range."

"Germans? At the missile range?"

Pandora smiled patiently. "They're West Germans, getting training in the operation of the missiles we've stationed in Western Europe."

"Hmm," Sam grunted. "Well, the beer should be good."

"When is this Oktoberfest?" J.B. wanted to know.

"Next weekend. Want to come along?"

"Sure. If Morgan and Sonny don't mind covering for me." He looked over at Morgan.

"It's fine with me. I'm not stir-crazy yet." J.B.'s face froze, but Morgan seemed oblivious to his choice of words. "We'll split your shift," he was saying.

"Yeah," Sam offered, "you two can go next year." They laughed at the prospect before them of another year and a half at White Sands.

"Terrific idea, Pandora," Sam concluded. "We'll have a great outing. I hope it's not as devastating to Arthur as the Fourth of July." He roared, and the others joined in.

Chapter 50

They took off in one of the wagons on Friday afternoon, Pandora driving, with Sam up front, and J.B., legs jackknifed, in the back with Bob. Heading south, they watched the San Andres drift away, then curve back, the clouds above mimicking the ragged outline of the peaks. The sweep of grass, bleached by the summer sun, thinned before them.

After ten miles, the buildings of the missile range appeared. J.B. studied them curiously. He had driven in at night with Pandora and seen nothing. So there really was a base here, with soldiers and scientists firing and tracking missiles above their heads. Their camp was not in the middle of nowhere, as Carl had described it, but in the middle of the field tests for the Third World War. For a moment, he regretted their jaunt into the real world.

They pulled up at a gate and Pandora showed identification to the soldier on guard. He peered in, more out of curiosity than duty, it seemed, then stepped back and waved them on. Pandora turned left onto the highway.

A neat row of mobile homes like their own marked the town of Organ. Then they were climbing sharply up to the pass through the mountains, and just as quickly, racing down the other side. They were in the flatlands again. The stillness beyond their windows suffocated conversation. But J.B., who was experiencing his first real excursion, beyond gates and fences, in three and a half years, soon became attuned to the subtle changes in the land. The red clay gave way to dark stony soil, sprinklings of yuccas displaced the tufts of grass, followed by the feathery branches of mesquite. Then the yuccas again, now planted in glistening white dunes of gypsum, as they cut through a corner of White Sands National Monument. He could feel the dunes, prodded by the wind, rising and collapsing with endless patience.

He turned to look eastward, surprised by a range of mountains that had emerged full-grown behind his back. The road widened and they sped down a tree-lined boulevard past the city of Alamogordo, a clump of low, adobe-colored buildings tucked under the mountains. A few miles farther on, they turned off the main highway and headed east, straight toward bare sculptured hills. The air cooled as they began climbing up into the Sacramento Mountains. The men rearranged their legs and shifted their weight. Sam relit his cigar.

Past ocatillo and small cactus they drove, winding through the greening hills. Piñon appeared, and then juniper, silvered with berries. Bob was ecstatic. He whipped his camera out of its case and began snapping, twisting in his seat in a vain effort to catch every perfect vista before it slipped by him.

"Slow down!" he yelled, but they were already passing a broad ledge that looked out, beyond prows of rock, to the basin below.

They drove through a short tunnel and came out into High Rolls, not a den of gamblers, but a community named for the dipping, twisting road, as they learned from the Chamber of Commerce brochures. Apple orchards and fields glided by. Across a chasm, a patch of aspen flamed among spruce and fir. Then a long horseshoe curve carried them into the village of Cloudcroft.

They negotiated the downtown area, distinguished by log cabins decorated with realtors' signs, in five minutes, slowed by the blue-jeaned groups that strolled across their path. A couple of schools and tennis courts later, they were once again among the pines and spruce.

"We must have missed something," Bob ventured.

They turned and, striking bravely off the main road this time, they followed a maze of narrow streets until a motel sign appeared.

"Looks clean," said Sam, and Pandora pulled over. After registering and leaving their bags in their rooms, they drove back to town and parked.

"Now what?" Sam demanded.

"Why don't we just follow the crowd?" J.B. suggested. And most of it did seem to be heading in the same direction. Ten minutes later they found themselves in the Alamo Bar.

Under the low rafters, in the dim light of the large room, they appraised their neighbors. Most of them were young Anglos. The regulars sat hunched around the bar, men and women wearing lumber jackets and klutzy boots, exuding the brave, arrogant aura of alternative life-stylers. Probably they eked out a living selling firewood and doing odd construction jobs. They came and went as if remembering important errands.

The visitors were more stylish and smiled more: couples in designer jeans, some of the men wearing a baby on their chest, the women gesturing with hands ringed with turquoise; groups of college kids. At one table, crew-cut Germans in civvies sat straight-backed, obviously on a break from a barracks.

The door swung wide as a covey of chicanas marched in. Enclosed in tight leather jackets, long black hair caught behind a headband, they headed for the ladies' room.

"Personally, I prefer the Club West," Sam remarked, after his second beer.

"Snob," Pandora reproached him.

"Actually," said Bob, "this isn't much different from the Club West. Why don't we walk around a little?"

They paid the tab and squeezed through the press.

Bob darted across the street to get a shot of the others leaving the Alamo, then rejoined them to peer into shop windows. After a few blocks, Sam was huffing.

"How high are we, anyway?"

"About nine thousand feet," Pandora answered.

After another block, they became aware that Sam was missing. They turned to see him leaning against one of the posts supporting the roof of the covered walk.

"I'm a navy man," he shouted, "not an eagle." He took a few breaths and asked sweetly, "Isn't it time we found a nice restaurant?"

Bob looked at his watch. "It's only six o'clock," he complained.

"Only the unimaginative are bound by schedules. Besides, it's past cocktail hour."

Pandora stopped someone who looked like a native, and then led the way to a hotel restaurant around the corner. Sam revived over a martini, and Bob consoled himself by poring over a brochure.

"Pandora! Good to see you."

They looked up into the smiling faces of Lieutenant Jenkins and a companion captain.

There were introductions all around and, as Jenkins continued to beam, and no one else seemed to recall the civilities of civilian life, Sam invited the two to join them.

The lieutenant dragged a chair toward Pandora. To avoid sitting next to him, J.B. made room for the other as well, and plunged into a minute examination of the menu.

Bob had returned to the brochure.

"The aspencade starts at eight tomorrow," he announced. "We gather at the Chamber of Commerce Building."

"Is that a hike?" Sam asked.

"No, no, we go in our own cars."

"Beautiful," Sam breathed.

"Yes," Howie agreed, "I hear it's really spectacular."

"We've both been looking forward to it," declared Jenkins. "Perhaps—if you don't think we're intruding—we could join you." He turned toward Pandora.

J.B. glanced at her, then returned to his menu. "That's a little early for me . . . since I'm on vacation."

"Yes," she agreed, "I'd like to see the exhibits."

"Why don't you take the wagon," J.B. suggested, addressing Bob and Sam, "and we'll just wander around."

"Fine," Bob chirped. "Then there'll be plenty of room for the lieutenant and his friend."

* * *

It was barely nine when they returned to their motel. J.B. yawned ostentatiously as he entered his room and closed the door. The bolt slid home with a crash.

He turned on the TV and waited about ten minutes. Then he gently retracted the bolt and stepped into the corridor. Pandora's room was two doors down.

"How come you got a room next to Bob's?" he asked sullenly.

"Because I think he's kind of cute," she said, putting her arms around his neck. "And because I didn't think I should fight him for the room adjoining yours."

"A likely story," he muttered, pulling her down on the bed. He was taking a great big gummy bite of her mouth when a voice intruded: ". . . with Maureen O'Hara and John Wayne." Pandora also had left the TV on.

He sat up. "We've got to watch this."

"What is it?"

"I haven't the slightest idea." He pulled off his clothes, tossing them toward a chair, and slipped under the covers. Pandora slowly followed, casting a baleful look at the screen. She softened as J.B., smiling, drew her close.

It was so ordinary, lying in bed watching the late show. And because of its ordinariness, so comforting. He felt connected to the world, freed of all fantasies, except perhaps the one being played out before them.

Long before the end of the late show, they fell asleep, his shoulder cradling her head, her arm around his neck.

Chapter 51

He awoke with Pandora's hand wrapped around him. They made love then.

Bob and Sam were long gone, and they ate a leisurely breakfast. It was the first time they had gone from bed to breakfast together, and the first time in public. They talked little, glances wandering, appraising the older couples and occasional family in the dining room, who appraised them, warming slowly under Bloody Marys.

They strolled the few blocks to the main street and fell in with the crowd. The air was cool under a sharp blue, cloudless sky, but they drew warmth from the closeness and gaiety of their neighbors.

Rows of booths led them into the small park. The sounds of a rock band overlay the chatter of the visitors as they fingered jewelry, tried on handwoven woolens and leather hats, stared at paintings of aspens and more aspens. Vendors of knives of all descriptions seemed to be doing well, as were the hot-dog and taco stands.

Gripping Pandora's hand, J.B. wandered over to a booth displaying silver and turquoise jewelry. His glance went down the rows of heavy belt buckles, skipped across the ornate concho belts, blurred at the dozens of rings, and came to rest on a pair of earrings shaped like tiny roses. He picked one up. A silver post extended from the back.

"Do you have pierced ears?"

She raised a hand to her ear. "Why—yes."

He held out his palm to the young Indian woman seated behind the table. "How much?"

"Twenty-five."

He let Pandora's hand drop and reached into his back pocket. He felt only the key to his room.

"God damn it," he whirled on Pandora, "how can I buy you something, woman, if I don't have any money?"

"J.B.," she began, "there's really no need—."

"This is absurd," he whispered to her, "I feel emasculated. Give me some money."

Pandora reached into her shoulder bag and dredged up a wallet. Looking right and left, she drew out a few bills and pressed them into his hand. He turned back to the woman, who was following his moves with mild amusement. He smiled and she reciprocated, taking the bills he counted out, glancing at Pandora.

"Thank you, ma'am," he said loudly, and scooped up the other earring.

"J.B., you don't have to," Pandora protested as they pushed into the crowd.

"I know I don't," he retorted, stopping to face her. "But I want to. Here."

She found another booth with a mirror. He watched her remove the gold hoops she wore and insert the silver roses. She raised her face to him.

"Beautiful," he pronounced, and kissed her on her nose.

She laughed as they moved on. "You *are* a romantic, J.B. What am I going to do with you?"

He smiled straight ahead. "Be gentle."

A game of horseshoes was in progress, and J.B. explained the scoring system. They cheered a wiry, bearded old man who made ringer after ringer.

At noon, aroused by the smells of the food booths, they lined up before one and bought sausage and sauerkraut and beer, and made their way cautiously to a bench.

A short, wide man in liederhose tilted his Tyrolean hat toward them as he stretched his accordion to an alarming length, producing a drawn-out yowl.

"Ach," J.B. grunted, "it reminds me of the beer garden we used to go to in my student days in Munich." He saluted the man with his beer and shouted, "Sig heil!" The accordionist grinned, but J.B.'s laugh was stifled by a resounding click behind them. They turned to see an elderly white-haired man, at stiff attention, his boot heels clamped together, drop his arm to his side. He seemed as startled as they. His mouth opened and then clamped shut. Abruptly he turned on his heel and marched into the crowd.

J.B. would have laughed but for the man's obvious distress. He peered through the crowd. The man reappeared and J.B. followed his progress through the maze of booths until he stopped at a beer stand. He leaned down to a shorter man and looked back toward them. J.B. stared at the face that now turned in their direction, the same face he thought he had recognized in the Cessna that morning after they had found the gold, the face in the photograph.

"What in Christ—," he spat out.

"What is it?" Pandora asked.

"I guess we've found Wild Bill Everett." When he looked back, the two men were gone.

What was Wild Bill doing now in Cloudcroft, he wondered. And what was he doing with that, that Nazi? For it seemed clear to J.B. that the man was an escapee from World War Two. His age was right, about sixty-eight or seventy. And his reaction to J.B.'s attempt at humor had been too severe, that of a man whose identity had been revealed.

What of himself? Had Wild Bill recognized him when they emerged from the cave, or here at the Oktoberfest? He must have. If so, he would be useless to the U.S. government. It wouldn't do for a fugitive from the law, a convicted murderer at that, to be found in the middle of the White Sands Missile Range.

Maybe he was useless now. He had successfully set up the project. The sabotage had been discovered and corrected. Now it was mostly a matter of maintenance, and he had trained Sonny and Morgan to run the operation. Maybe he ought to stop planning and just escape while he could.

There seemed little point in pursuing Wild Bill. They'd never find him in the crowd. And by the same token, they were practically invisible to Wild Bill. Still, he found himself glancing over his shoulder from time to time. The frown hovered around the corners of his mouth throughout the afternoon.

They walked slowly back toward downtown Cloudcroft and found a restaurant for dinner. Halfway through the barbecued ribs, a country and western band took up position by the dance floor.

"I haven't been stomp-dancing in years," J.B. exclaimed, brightening. And when the music started, they wound their way to the polished floor.

He felt like a clod, but loosened up after a few numbers, an expert among the floppy-armed young rock and rollers who surrounded them. Pandora, smoothly following him, was delighted.

They sealed the evening with a glass of peppermint schnapps. He called for the check and tossed some bills on the table. What a pleasure to have money in his pocket. It made him feel—competent.

He pushed open the door and they sidestepped a couple coming in. The chill wrapped itself around them. They sniffed and shivered and she moved closer as he put his arm around her waist.

"Which way?" he asked. "You're the navigator."

She pointed. "Over there, I think."

"Let's take a shortcut. I want to get you in a dark alley."

She giggled and let him lead her between the restaurant and a darkened shop.

"It's not really an alley," said J.B., "but it'll have to do." He stopped, and in the scant light of a sliver of old moon, they kissed.

The crackle of a shoe on paper made them draw apart. "It'll do just fine, J.B." The hairs on the back of his neck prickled at the low voice.

"You're out late, Wild Bill," J.B. said dryly, turning back toward the man. He eased Pandora behind him.

Wild Bill chuckled. "Yeah, both of us."

"I'm surprised to see you still in the state." He lit a cigarette, casually, he thought, and saw the glint of metal waist-high. It disappeared.

"Well, I was real lucky, J.B. I was on my way to El Paso, and I met up with this dude, and he offered me a job. Didn't ask too many questions or nothing."

"The Nazi," J.B. said.

There was another low chuckle. "Otto's not a bad guy. Been pretty good to me. I don't ask too many questions, either." He took two slow steps forward. "He tells me you been up to some interesting tricks."

"Such as?"

"Drilling for oil at White Sands."

"That's nonsense."

"That's not what Otto says. He says you're planning to go all the way to Iran."

J.B. forced a laugh. "That's dumb. That's just an old joke."

"Well, that's what I thought, but Otto seems to know a lot about you. Got a real good picture of you from a plane one day. Says you been in the oil business and know a lot about that stuff. He followed your friend up to Los Alamos a couple of times. Says you're doing it with lasers."

"Then—he was the one who—?"

"Nah, that was me in the pickup."

J.B. was tired of games. "And?"

"Well, the folks Otto works for aren't going to like that a bit. Might make the Ayatollah a little testy, you know what I mean?"

"Fuck the Ayatollah." With thumb and middle finger, J.B. shot the cigarette at Wild Bill and lunged for his knees. They rolled over, pummeling each other. The gun thudded against the ground. J.B. grunted when a fist slammed into his kidney. Wild Bill was not too smart, but he was solid.

They rolled against a garbage can and the clatter caught the brief attention of passersby. "Drunks," someone called, laughing.

They were both panting now. J.B. felt they'd been struggling for half an hour. He couldn't keep it up much longer. He wasn't in shape. There were too many years encircling his waist. Wild Bill clipped him on the chin and his head bounced on the ground. He kicked out but Wild Bill was leaning away from him, scrabbling for his gun.

There was a soft whistle, almost a sneeze. Wild Bill collapsed. A gurgle broke the stillness.

J.B., with difficulty, pushed him over. Blood bubbled at his neck, then stopped. He looked back toward Pandora. She was on her knees, the tiny gun clenched in her right hand.

He stood up slowly, his legs wobbly, and took a step toward her. She didn't move. "You all right?" he whispered.

It was enough to melt the glue she had dredged up to hold herself together. She let him pull her up and then fell into his arms.

"It's all right. Don't cry."

"I'm not crying," she said, pulling away slightly so he could see her face. "It's just—." She shuddered. "I've never done that before."

J.B. smiled sadly. "I guess," he drawled, "we all do what we have to do."

She closed her eyes and nodded, unaware of his eyes crawling over her mouth, her nose, her fluttering lashes.

Yes, Pandora, he thought, we're all capable of that final outrage, that ultimate violation.

Chapter 52

Pandora pleaded a badly upset stomach the next morning, to persuade Sam and Bob to cut short their outing and return to White Sands.

"Christ, Pandora, it was your idea. We've only been here one day," Bob reproached her.

"Ah, I kind of miss Alfie's cooking," Sam countered. "All this wurst and beer is getting to me, too."

They checked out after breakfast and the men dutifully ducked into the wagon when Pandora drove it up. She was quiet but composed on the ride back.

"You should have come along on the aspencade. I shot five rolls of film," Bob declared. "We had a great time, didn't we, Sam?"

"Yah, we had a ball."

"What'd you guys do?" Bob asked.

"Oh, we just wandered around," J.B. replied. He shifted in the back seat and caught Pandora's grave face in the rear-view mirror.

"Did you guys see that Nazi?"

The car swerved, and Pandora looked apologetically toward Sam. He flipped a cigar stub out the window.

"They were all Nazis, as far as I'm concerned."

"No, no," Bob argued, "this one looked like something right out of Central Casting. Tall, straight as an arrow." He paused to laugh and leer meaningfully at J.B. "Kind of arrogant, you know? We passed him, coming back from the aspencade."

"I think we missed him," J.B. responded quietly.

Pandora concentrated on the curving road. Once the mountain wall opened up and they glimpsed the dunes of White Sands. Then they were driving by them, down in the flatlands again.

They stopped at the gate of the missile range. The young guard, less blasé than the first, narrowed his eyes at Pandora.

"Yes, ma'am," he said, leaning on the door, "what can I do for you?" She showed him her papers. He looked up at her expressionless face, down to the papers again, and handed them back, waving her on. He stood there in the driveway, looking after her and the wagon until they curved around a hill that obliterated him.

"What do those papers of yours say, anyway, Pandora?" Sam wanted to know.

"Q clearance," Bob offered, "admit anywhere." He giggled. Pandora remained silent.

Half an hour later, they pulled up in front of the Washington Club West. Sam turned to Pandora, extending his hand.

"I had a lovely time. Thank you, ma'am."

* * *

"Do you have to report it?"

"What? Yes." Her eyes were riveted to the television screen on which two attendants were carrying the green-bagged corpse of Wild Bill Everett. State prison officials seemed not to consider the demise of Donald William Everett untimely. They were relieved one of their escapees would not be out raping and pillaging. Only one of the men who had escaped in the spring was still at large, the reporter noted—J.B. Craddock. Prison authorities had no idea of his whereabouts.

J.B. glanced at Pandora. Would they start hunting for him in the southern part of the state, since Wild Bill had shown up here? Well, he was safe at White Sands. Or was he? What if they found the Nazi? Or he found them? Not likely. But—.

"What's going to happen to Straight Arrow now?" he wondered aloud.

"I don't know," Pandora answered, turning from the set. "If it's true he's working for Iran—and we have no reason to doubt it—and if our people can't neutralize him—I suppose it might be dangerous to continue the project."

J.B. marveled at her. She was her usual calm, cool self again, seemingly untroubled by her "neutralization" of Wild Bill. Change the words and you can change the feelings. Eliminate the word "kill" and you can eliminate guilt, eliminate—anyone. Is that what he had done to Marybelle, neutralized her? No. Perhaps.

He felt very tired. "I'm going to turn in early," he said from the doorway. "See you tomorrow."

Chapter 53

"Have a good time in Cloudcroft?"

J.B. had barely nodded to Morgan when he came down the steps into the lab the next morning.

"Oh, yeah. It was terrific," he said, but the flatness of his tone made Morgan stop and look him over.

"Hope you and Sonny didn't work too hard."

Morgan smiled sourly. "Don't we wish."

J.B. plopped into the chair at the console. "Seriously, thanks for standing in for me."

Morgan raised his hand to stop him. "Don't worry about it. Sonny and I plan to get even at Christmas. Figure we'll fly down to Puerto Vallarta for a couple of days."

J.B., eyes wide, followed Morgan's back up the stairs. He was chuckling. Son of a gun, thought J.B., he's got a sense of humor after all.

He soon fell back into his preoccupied state, rousing himself only to take a spectrograph from time to time. It had been too good to be true. Everything had gone so smoothly. Well, except for Straight Arrow's having taken that wrong turn, of course. Now this business in Cloudcroft. He should have asked Wild Bill about the computer.

The picture of the Nazi, hand half-raised in that absurd but frightening gesture, oppressed him. Well, maybe they'd get him, Pandora's playmates, that is. But he remained uneasy.

There was one bright spot, one golden gleam of hope—the treasure. A solution to the problem of carrying it out still eluded him, but he was sure they'd find a way. It was more important than ever now. They were scheduled to bring the laser up on Friday. After that, they'd have another break, time to get down to it and make some plans.

The jeep sat like a gauntlet thrown in his path, in front of Pandora's trailer, when he emerged from the lab on Wednesday. He glowered at it, as if staring it down could make it disappear. It refused to move.

He thought of driving it into one of the arroyos that snaked through the missile range. No, that would only prolong Lieutenant Jenkins' visit.

He spat and retreated to his quarters.

* * *

"I'm sure it's the same man," Jenkins was saying. "I've seen his picture on the news twice now—I remembered, when I saw it the other night, that I'd seen it earlier this year—that's why he looked so familiar to me."

Pandora tilted her head to one side and tried to smile. "Now, Tim, you know that's absurd; what would a murderer be doing here?" she asked reasonably.

"I haven't the foggiest," said Tim, "but I know he's a dangerous man."

"Well, I saw that picture, too, and the man on TV had a beard. He's at least ten years older than Jim."

Jenkins shook his head. "It was just a few days' growth of stubble, and that made him look older. That, and his circumstances, I'm sure. I know it's the same man."

"And I'm sure you're mistaken," Pandora countered.

Jenkins frowned. "Don't you realize the danger you're in, Pandora? He *killed* a woman—his girlfriend, or wife, or whatever. It was in the papers, after the escape."

Pandora rose and moved to the window and stared out. "Jim is a technician here, with a job to do."

"Yes, and I don't understand how he got through a security check. He really put one over on—somebody."

"Exactly," Pandora pronounced, turning. "You don't understand what's going on here, and, of course, I can't tell you."

The lieutenant paused. "Somebody's got to do something. I feel responsible now."

Pandora sighed. "You are not responsible. *I* am responsible. Now . . . just forget it."

"No . . . it's not right . . . it's my duty . . . ." he mumbled.

Pandora rolled her eyes up to the ceiling. "I'll take care of it," she said, dropping down beside him on the couch. "I promise you, I'll look into it."

"When?"

"Immediately."

"And you'll let me know tomorrow, or the next day?"

"I'll let you know in a week—two weeks."

"We can't let this slide, Pandora."

"You'll hear from me in two weeks."

Chapter 54

Carl was there early Friday, as reliable as the sun coming up in the morning and just as cheerful. He had finally broken down and acquired a straw western hat. He shook J.B.'s hand warmly and strode over to the lab with him.

"You know, we're really very proud of you, J.B.," he beamed. "Everyone thinks you're doing a magnificent job."

"I appreciate that, Carl," J.B. responded. And he did. Accomplishment was comforting, and he had gone too long without a sense of it. He hoped only that the praise would continue until he was ready to take his leave.

Carl paused to look over the mounds of vaporized rock. "We'll have to start carting that stuff away." He turned back to J.B. "How far have we gone now?"

"Five hundred and eighty miles." He examined the toes of his boots. "Of course, we went another hundred miles on that detour."

Carl squeezed his shoulder. "Don't worry about it. It's still fantastic."

J.B. and Sonny moved the winch into place, and they began the process of rolling up the cables as the laser backed up. Carl watched for a few minutes before excusing himself.

Slowly the spools outside the trailer grew fat. The men broke for dinner at six, then went back to work. J.B. called a halt at midnight. Gratefully, Sonny and Morgan tramped up the stairs. After shutting down the computer and generator, J.B. followed.

Alfie fed them steak and eggs the next morning, and they resumed at nine. It wasn't until midnight that the dusty body of Straight Arrow appeared. Carl drove it away early Sunday.

A few hours later, J.B. appeared at Pandora's door. "Let's take a walk. Maybe we'll get some ideas on the site."

Pandora hesitated. "Aren't you exhausted?"

He grinned. "Sure, but I know just the thing to perk me up—the sight of those dirty black bars."

They were on their way in fifteen minutes, after cajoling Alfie into preparing another picnic basket—minus all the jars. "Just some sandwiches, Alfie, and a couple of canteens of water."

"I don't know what you folks see out there that's so fascinating," Alfie grumbled. He looked up brightly. "Maybe it's just that it feels so good to get back, huh?"

"Right!" they laughed.

They walked north for a half hour and stopped. J.B. studied the low hills of the Sierra Caballos on the west, then scoured the San Andres Mountains.

"This way," he said, taking a tangent to the northeast.

"Are you sure? This isn't the way we went before."

"Should take a few miles off." He trudged decisively over the hillocks, and Pandora gave herself up to his direction. Occasionally he looked back toward the Caballos, aligning a peak with one of the San Andres. After an hour, they were in the eastern foothills. In the spotty shade of a clump of mesquite, they sat and ate Alfie's sandwiches.

"Not as interesting as the first time around," J.B. complained, picking at a piece of lettuce that overhung the bread.

"Nothing is, I suppose," she smiled.

He paused at the hint of nostalgia in her voice. He studied the dark eyelashes as she bent down to her sandwich, the straight line of her nose, the triangle of creamy flesh exposed by her shirt.

She caught him watching her. He leaned forward, wrapping his hand around her knee, and glowered at her. "What did you mean by that?"

She laughed and gripped the hand gripping her knee. "Don't read more into something than there is," she admonished him.

He scooted forward until his face was a foot away from hers. "Pandora," he said, "you do want to run away with me, don't you?"

Her smile faded. "Yes, J.B., I would like to run away with you." Would. Do. He grunted and snaked back to his place. Don't read any more into that than there is, he told himself.

Half a canteen of water later, they were climbing up into the mountains, although their progress seemed more horizontal. Had it been this rocky and circuitous before? Soon enough they had emerged into the basin, the isolated peak before them. J.B. looked back toward the mountain wall for reference. It was somewhere around here, he frowned, he was sure of it.

Grass had begun to smooth the edges, but the big metal doors slid into their consciousness like a gate slamming shut. Buzz, clang. It was the doors of the state pen again, closing off escape.

"Is this the right place?" he cried.

Pandora looked around them. "I think so."

He tried to get a grip on one door, but they were welded shut, hinged to stout timbers sunk into the ground.

"I don't believe it," he said. "Where did this come from? Who's been out here?" He sank back on his haunches.

"That plane," Pandora said, "that jet that ran off the light plane. Maybe it came back. To see what we were doing here."

God damn it. "God damn it to hell," he said aloud. "But why would they close it up like this?"

"To keep people out," Pandora said reasonably. "To keep them from getting the gold."

J.B. sighed deeply. "Or maybe to keep people from knowing they had taken the gold out!" They stared at each other.

"But surely we would have heard about it, J.B., if the army had found all that gold. On the news."

"Would we?"

"What would the army do with it? They would have to report it—."

He snorted. "Report what to whom? They could simply build a few more nuclear bombs with it. A few more 'Peacekeeper' missiles."

Pandora frowned. "I don't understand. But there must be a logical explanation for it."

J.B. leaned forward, hands outstretched on the rock. "Logical. Yes. They've killed our chances to get away."

She knelt beside him and rubbed his back. "Don't feel so bad. You'll find another way." He reached behind and sought her hand, and she slipped it into his. Do I read too much into things, he wondered, or not enough. Suddenly his back went rigid.

"What is it?"

He was reaching out before him, digging something out of the dirt. He held it up, a small round gold-plated medal. He snickered. He had always wondered what the inscription was. It read, "The Golden Eagle Club." The president's elite group of fundraisers.

"Well," he said, rising and holding it out in his hand. "We may not know why. But we do know who."

Chapter 55

Arthur raised his hands helplessly. "I can't imagine how they found out, Mr. President, but, of course, there are spies and blackguards everywhere."

The president winced. Arthur was a bit old-fashioned. But then he seemed to have the military under control, and there were fewer cries of waste and mismanagement from legislators and columnists these days.

"You say the Nazi escaped?"

"Yes," Arthur flexed his fingers, "slipped right through our hands. Of course, the project is compromised now."

"Yes," the president agreed reluctantly, "I suppose so. Seems like an awful waste."

"Not so much as you think, Mr. President," Arthur hurriedly explained, "less than six hundred thousand dollars, I believe."

"A bargain."

"Yes, I would say so." Arthur never quite knew when the president was serious and when he was being sarcastic.

The president stuck the top of his pen in his mouth. "You'll take care of that geologist, I trust. He did, after all, do his best for us."

"Of course, Mr. President, we'll take care of everything."

Chapter 56

J.B. ran his fingertips over the gleaming white carapace of Straight Arrow. Not bad. Not bad at all for an old boy from the oil patch. Let's hope this isn't the last time we send you down the hole.

He fitted the laser into the mouth of the tunnel and started the generator and the computer. The laser glided down. Then he moved the ruby laser into place and checked the direction of Straight Arrow. It was right on target.

He went outside, past the heaps of rubble, to where Sonny and Morgan were uncoiling cables from one of the spools.

"I'll switch with one of you, if you want." Morgan shrugged. Sonny took off his gloves and tossed them to J.B. "I'd rather be down in the pit. Thanks, J.B."

They worked quietly, paying out the lines rhythmically. As the sun rose, they took off their light jackets and tossed them on the ground. J.B. had hoped Sonny would remain outside. He never had much to say to Morgan, and the monotony of the job cried for diversion.

"You missed a great dance in Cloudcroft," J.B. threw out.

Morgan grinned at him. "Thanks, old buddy."

"Yeah, there were all these sweet young things in tight jeans, stomping their little hearts out."

"I'm not much for dancing, myself."

"What do you do out here for recreation? Must be hard on a young guy like you."

Morgan glanced at him slyly. "You seem to do all right."

J.B. felt his face redden. "Yes. Well. I'm the gregarious type. I tag along with Bob when he goes out snapping pictures, play backgammon with Pandora, whatever."

"I hear that backgammon's a pretty tricky game."

"It keeps your mind occupied."

J.B. exhaled deeply and tried to concentrate on the cables. Discipline, he thought, that's what I need. Morgan has discipline. He watched the other man steadily feeding the cables back down into the lab. His arms were slim but muscular. Muscles quivered under his T-shirt. And he had no beer belly.

"How do you stay in shape, Morgan?"

"Pushups, mostly. Sometimes I jog."

"Around here?"

"In the evening, sometimes. When it's not too hot."

Funny, J.B. thought, he'd never noticed Morgan out jogging. But then he hadn't noticed much since he'd started keeping company with Pandora.

"You married?"

"No . . . I like peace and quiet."

J.B. capitulated. Why was it, he wondered, that whenever he embarked on a conversation with Morgan, the other man learned more about him than he did about Morgan? Must be some failing in himself.

All right, loose lips, he said to himself, discipline.

Chapter 57

For three days they continued operating as before, taking their regular shifts, cursing the heat, cracking stale jokes with Alfie. Then Arthur appeared. He called Pandora, Sam and Bob into the club for a conference, sending Alfie to fetch J.B.

"Oh, and Alfie," he added, "take a break for an hour or so."

"Sure, chief," Alfie responded.

"The big man's here," Alfie told J.B. "Told me to get lost for a while, while you guys have a conference."

J.B. raised his eyebrows. He hesitated a moment, then turned off the computer and the generator. He squeezed Alfie's shoulder as he headed for the stairs.

"He *is* a tactful son-of-a-bitch, isn't he? Don't worry. You're probably not missing much." J.B. didn't believe that for a minute.

They were silent when he entered and took a seat. Arthur rose. He clamped his hands behind his back and took a stance so that he could face both J.B. and Pandora.

"Well, you two had a merry time in Cloudcroft." They waited, silent. "Under the circumstances, we are, of course, aborting Project Straight Arrow."

J.B. and Pandora looked down guiltily. Sam and Bob were outraged.

"What the hell—," Sam began.

"What do you mean? It's going perfectly!" Bob protested.

Arthur turned to gaze at them. He seemed somehow different, J.B. thought, incomplete. Ah, yes, his lapel pin was missing.

"What's going on, Arthur?" Sam demanded.

"It seems we've been spied upon. A former Nazi working for Iran. Pandora shot his cohort in Cloudcroft—an old friend of J.B.'s—but the Nazi got away." He glanced at J.B. "Of course we can't continue now. Iran would make an awful row. There would be an international furor."

Bob looked accusingly at Pandora. "You never said a word. Why didn't you tell us?"

"There was really no point," Pandora murmured.

Sam lit a fresh cigar and leaned back. "Well, it was too good to last, I suppose."

"The president wants you and Bob to return to Washington immediately," Arthur said. He turned to Pandora. "And your job is over now."

Pandora stiffened. "I haven't been officially recalled."

"A matter of a day or two, I imagine."

Gloom settled over the room like ash from a volcano. They had been a cheerful group for the most part, an exclusive club, bonded by the secrecy and excitement of their mission, outrageous as it had at first appeared. Now they were crestfallen. J.B. thought of Carl's enthusiasm, his unrelenting good humor. He started at the sound of his name.

"What about J.B.?" Sam had asked.

"We're working on that," Arthur replied. "We'll get him a new identity and history and set him up somewhere . . . ." he trailed off. J.B. couldn't help making a sour face.

"In the meantime, he and Morgan and Sonny will help wrap things up here. I'll speak to them personally." He fingered his lapel absentmindedly.

"Well, that's all," Arthur dismissed them. "Unless there are any questions." There were no questions.

They straggled out of the trailer as Alfie came up. He looked at their faces quizically. "What happened? Somebody die?"

J.B. regarded him for a moment. "Not yet." But, of course, that's what they were planning. J.B. would die. He would become someone else, a new "identity." The prospect did not please him.

From his window, later, he saw Arthur talking to Morgan. The younger man looked toward J.B.'s trailer and nodded. Then Arthur walked in the direction of Sonny's quarters. Morgan watched him go, before disappearing from view.

Chapter 58

J.B. was loathe to bring up Straight Arrow. He didn't want to see it lying there on the steel floor of the lab like a beached whale. For all his doubts, he had committed himself to the project. It represented a significant chunk of his energy and thought. He resisted acknowledging the end of it.

"Why don't we postpone it until tomorrow?" he suggested to Morgan and Sonny. "Arthur said there was no hurry. And you two have been working steadily for five months. Take a rest and then we'll get down to it."

Sonny shrugged. "It's all the same to me. But I suppose I can take some more of this easy life," he smiled. Morgan agreed.

J.B. realized it was not just the end of Straight Arrow that he didn't want to face. He was also reluctant to talk to Pandora. She had said they would find another way, without the gold. But there was so little time now to work things out. He wasn't sure he wanted to know what she was thinking.

He avoided her for most of the day before deciding to take the plunge.

"They've given me a week to get back," she said, after letting him in. "I told them I needed some time . . . ." He turned to face her.

"Are you going?"

She sat down in the chair opposite the sofa and licked the corner of her mouth. "I don't know."

He went into the kitchen and returned with a bottle of sour mash and two glasses. He poured out drinks and handed her a glass. She took it gingerly, barely looking at him. He took a swallow and leaned forward on the couch.

"I know it's not the way we thought it would be. No fortune to take us wherever we want to go. But we do have that one bar. And I know I can get a job in Mexico."

She turned the glass in her hands. Her forehead creased. "It sounded so . . . easy, before. We'd have had security. Now, I don't know. It would be like starting life all over, with nothing."

"But each other," he added quietly.

"I do love you," she said.

"I know." He felt the old tightness in his chest, spreading upward into his throat. He wanted to touch her. But he remained seated.

She took a sip of her drink. "I'm not very adventurous, J.B. I mean, this sounds like an exciting job, but it's really pretty cut and dried. Most of the time. They teach you all the right reflexes, and it's automatic. You don't have to think about them much . . . ."

I wish someone would teach me the right reflexes, he thought. He forced himself up, going to her side and kissing her lightly on her forehead. She reached for his hand.

"There's still some time," she said. "I really don't know what I should do."

He squeezed her hand and withdrew, setting his glass on the table. "You're right," he said at the door. "We'll have some time to think about it." But time, he felt, was quickening.

Chapter 59

Sam came to say good-bye.

"Take care of yourself, kid," he advised, growling around a cigar. "Make sure they fix you up with something decent. Stay away from Arizona."

J.B. laughed. He had heard of talkative mobsters who had gone to Arizona, supposedly with clean new identities, who had died unexpectedly and, often, explosively there.

"Thanks, Sam," he said, grasping the man's outstretched hand.

"And, uh, don't believe everything Arthur says. He's a very practical patriot." J.B. nodded.

"You take care of the president," he said. "Sounds like he needs all the help he can get."

"Yeah," Sam mused, "politics is as bad as the TV ratings game." He pursed his lips. "I guess it *is* the TV ratings game."

They both chuckled as J.B. followed him to the door. "I guess it's none of my business," J.B. added, "but . . . it's too bad things didn't work out between you and Lilly Mae."

Sam turned. "Oh, she's coming down to Washington next week. Says she owes it to herself to get a first-hand look at the den of iniquity."

Bob was already in the jeep that had come for them, looking calm and detached, like a man who had finally found his own path. He had confided earlier that he was going back to St. Louis to open a photography studio and, perhaps, back to Lila.

Arthur was pacing alongside. "Well, come on, come on," he urged Sam. "The business of the nation isn't going to wait."

"The country's really fortunate to have you for a public servant," Sam observed, climbing into the vehicle. Arthur snorted and thrust out his hand to J.B.

"We'll be in touch," he said brusquely, and ducked into the right front seat. J.B. couldn't reply. The glint of gold on Arthur's lapel had stunned him.

He walked through the dust churned up by the rear wheels and hurried back to his trailer.

Where had he put that damn Boy Scout pin? Top drawer of the dresser. No, second. He pulled it out and rummaged around. No, top. He pulled out the top drawer. It was gone. Of course it's gone, you dummy, Arthur is wearing it.

But who had taken it? He couldn't imagine Arthur rifling the shirts and shorts Pandora had so fastidiously selected. Was there another agent in their midst?

Morgan. Morgan? Who else? He had always thought Morgan a little bizarre.

My God. He hurried to the bathroom and raised the lid of the tank. The gold brick was still there.

One more place to check. He pulled a boot out of the closet, tapped the toe and turned it over. Out fell the tiny diamond-edged saw blade. He squatted there, trying to think. Maybe they hadn't searched the whole place, probably just looking for the pin. But when he rose and looked around, it seemed the hair comb lay not quite at the angle at which he had left it, a box of tissues had moved an inch. He felt exposed.

When? When had he had the time to get in here? Oh. When he had gone to talk with Pandora.

Pandora. Had she known all this time that Morgan was an agent? Why hadn't she told him? Why did they need two of them out here?

"Why didn't you tell me Morgan was an agent?"

Pandora, wrapped in a towel and half hidden behind the door, stared at him. "Morgan?"

J.B. slammed the door behind him and marched into the living room, recounting the discovery of Arthur's pin—on Arthur, and the search of his quarters.

Hugging the towel to her, Pandora followed him as far as the sofa. "That doesn't seem possible, J.B."

"What do you mean?" he snapped.

"I saw Morgan go out jogging just before you came over—the first time."

J.B., deflated, slumped into the chair. "Then who the hell searched my place? That doesn't seem like Arthur's line."

She perched on the arm of the sofa, pondering.

"Alfie? Bob?" he asked sarcastically. "Hardly likely."

"Certainly not Sam," she said. "That leaves Sonny."

"Sonny?" he asked, incredulous. "That sweet all-American kid?"

She shrugged. "I don't know."

"How come you didn't know there was someone else out here?"

"I don't know," she repeated, wavering between anger and alarm.

"Maybe you're all a bunch of spies."

"Maybe you're just a smart-ass ladykiller with delusions of your own importance!"

He sat down and dropped his forehead into his hand. "I'm sorry."

"Me too."

They were silent for a time. J.B. considered Sonny, then Morgan. He didn't like not knowing who his enemies were. He could probably count on Arthur. But Sonny?

"When was the last time you saw the pin?"

"I hadn't noticed it for days. Not until I saw it on Arthur."

"Someone could have taken it while Arthur was talking to us."

"And both Sonny and Morgan were absent from that meeting."

"Strange," Pandora mused, "when I told them I needed a few days before going back to Washington, they said, 'We're covered.' I didn't think to ask what they meant."

"Why do you think they planted someone else here?"

Pandora wrapped the towel tighter. "Maybe they didn't trust me to handle the job." She frowned. "Maybe there was something else they didn't think I could handle."

J.B. clasped his hands and leaned forward, looking at her steadily. "Do you think they planned from the start to kill me?"

"No one's tried to kill you, J.B.," she objected. "But . . . Arthur always seemed disturbed by the possibility of your name becoming linked with the president's."

"And now," he added, "he knows that I know that he's got millions in gold stashed away somewhere."

They watched the light fade outside, each thinking thoughts he didn't want to put into words.

Finally Pandora moved. "Do you want some dinner?" she asked.

"No. I'm not very hungry. I don't think I'd be very good company, anyway."

Chapter 60

The moon was a smile, casting a wordless benediction over the plain. J.B., sitting on the step of his trailer, caught his breath. It came to him that life was very precious. He thought of Marybelle. For the first time, he cried for her.

Why had he killed her?

He had had a few drinks, but he knew that was no excuse. She had betrayed him, but the word tasted sour on his tongue. He hadn't really been in love with her. Theirs had been a union of mindless convenience. Ego? That was the world's mirror. He had never been overly concerned with what others thought of him, with proving himself to them.

He watched the moon rise steadily, illuminating a small patch of sky around it, inserting its pale glow into the dark.

Marybelle had thrown a cold light on his seamless days. She had forced him to wonder what he was doing living with a dumb broad in a backwater town, working at a dead-end job that paid just enough to keep him coming back. And when he could come up with no satisfactory answer, he had tried to wring one out of her.

Dumb broad. An easy expletive to avoid thinking, self-reproach. Of course Marybelle was not dumb. She had simply chosen to cultivate beauty instead of brains. And in truth, a Marybelle who displayed brains would have scared hell out of most men. He thought now she had been rather astute at keeping him around as long as it pleased her. Had it no longer pleased her?

No matter. He sickened at the thought of the wasted years, his clinging to a gray security. How had he ever gotten off his own track? Where had he misplaced that dream, in the top drawer? Under the shorts? He couldn't even remember what it was.

Marybelle had broken the pattern he had constructed for and around himself, that skein of rituals and habit he had woven that passed for life, and he hated her for it.

Now another pattern was splintering. First the Nazi, then Arthur, and now even Pandora had fractured the cozy routine he had built in the desert, that was to have had its culmination in a golden deliverance with Pandora at his side. He couldn't fault her. She was doing what she wanted to do, helping to contain the evils of the world. If she ever relaxed her guard, she would let loose a host of plagues. No matter that the plagues might be within her.

She had toyed with the prospect of running away with him. But he realized now that, even had the gold been accessible to them, she could not have gone through with it.

And what was he running away from? Well, of course, there was that business of his being an escaped convict; and now it seemed there might be someone out there in the yuccas planning to kill him. Yes, those were respectable reasons for running. But it was about time he found something to run to, besides another comfortable web of delusion.

Chapter 61

They started bringing up the laser the next day, but J.B.'s heart was not in it.

"There's no sense wearing ourselves out," he told Morgan and Sonny. "We can work five hours a day, and have it up in about a week."

They agreed, and the three men settled into an easy routine, taking occasional breaks. At noon they stopped to have lunch together at the club. There was little talk, and Alfie eventually abandoned all attempts to humor them.

Pandora hovered round them at first, but there seemed no need for her vigilance, and after a day or two she relaxed and returned to her old inconspicuous ways.

A day later they were interrupted by the distant groan and grind of motors. Slogging toward them was a front-end loader leading two dump trucks.

"What's all that for?" Sonny wondered.

"I know," said Alfie, "they're going to shovel us up, trailers and all, so there won't be a trace left in White Sands."

Sonny and Morgan laughed, but J.B. was uncomfortable with Alfie's words.

"Actually," he said, "I think you're pretty close. They're probably going to cart off all the debris we've been accumulating."

On the far side of the lab, mountains of vaporized rock squatted. The vehicles rolled up to them, followed by J.B. and the others. The three drivers climbed down. The loader operator planted his hands on his hips and looked over the rock.

"I guess this is the mess we're supposed to clean up."

"Right," J.B. said. "What are you going to do with it?"

"Spread it around here and there." He turned and looked in all directions. "Mostly around those hills, I guess," he said, pointing to the San Andres Mountains. "It won't stick out so much there."

A belated idea flashed through J.B.'s mind. God, that would have been just the thing to take out the gold, a dump truck covered with rock, and a ready-made excuse for it. Too bad.

The men climbed back into their trucks and went to work. J.B. went below, leaving Sonny and Morgan to coil the cables. But the noise was too much for them. Soon Morgan stuck his head through the trap door.

"Let's take a break!" he shouted. J.B. was relieved someone else had suggested it.

At four o'clock the newcomers quit for the day. As the rattles and groans of machinery dissipated, J.B. and the others emerged from their burrows.

"We were told there were some mobile homes we could use," the loader operator said.

J.B. pointed out Sam's and Bob's quarters. "And that's the chuck wagon over there," he added, pointing out the Washington Club West. The three drivers shambled away.

Judging from the inconsequential dent they had made in the rock pile, J.B. estimated they would be around for a week.

"I guess we'll just have to wait until they finish every day, and then go to work."

Morgan shook his head. "That's going to play hell with my TV-watching." Sonny and J.B. laughed, as he walked toward the door of the lab. "My turn down in the hole?"

"Why not?"

They worked silently for an hour, but Sonny seemed uncharacteristically restless. J.B. noticed him glancing up occasionally at the loader, whose crane towered above the lab. J.B. stopped and looked at him questioningly.

He snickered. "Those things have always turned me on, you know? Like a kid with an electric train . . . or nowadays, with Pac-Man. You sit up there with all those levers and everything moves so smoothly." He pulled a coil of cable around the spool. "I guess it's the power you have, moving that bucket around."

J.B. nodded, setting to work again.

"I was up in one of them when I was a kid," Sonny continued. He looked around. No one else was in sight. The drivers were probably in the club, being charmed by Alfie.

"Hey," he breathed, "I'm going to get up there. Just for a minute," and he started around the end of the lab.

J.B., frowning, hurried after him. "Those guys might not like someone playing with their toys," he suggested.

"It's OK, I can handle it," Sonny assured him.

J.B. was at a loss. He wasn't really in charge here, and he didn't like playing boss, but he knew one didn't fool around with heavy equipment.

"Uh. People can get hurt in those things, Sonny," he warned.

Sonny was climbing up into the cab. He turned to look down at J.B. "Don't *worry*, I know what I'm *doing*," he emphasized, as if speaking to a child. J.B. sighed and folded his arms on his chest.

Sonny started up the motor. The roar vibrated through J.B., but no one else seemed to hear it. The loader backed hesitantly and turned and moved slowly toward one of the hills of dirt. Well, J.B. conceded to himself, he does seem to know what he's doing.

The shovel rose, stopped, rose again. It dug into the dirt slowly and ascended once more, closing. A lever groaned and the loader turned. The shovel opened and spewed a stream of rock neatly onto another pile. J.B. looked over to the cab. Sonny was beaming at him.

He lowered the shovel and turned the loader. Again the shovel bit into the dirt and swung up smoothly. The loader turned on its tracks. The shovel released its load. Pac-Man was a good analogy, J.B. thought. The kid is mesmerized. He shook his head and turned away. I give up. Better tell Morgan we've had it for the evening.

Morgan was just coming around the other end of the lab, irritated by the cables piling up below. "What's going on?" he called.

Fun and games in the desert, he was about to say, when Morgan's expression stopped him. He started to turn as a spray of dirt dusted his head.

He felt a smashing blow and thought at first that the shovel had dropped a ton of dirt on him. But it was only his ribs that hurt. Morgan, running, had shoved him out of the way and now was sprawled beside him on the ground. They lay there panting as much from surprise as from the exertion.

Sonny was on top of them in a second.

"Are you guys all right?" he cried, his eyes wide as he reached for J.B.'s arm, his leg. They nodded slowly. "Jesus, I don't know what happened! I swear I was turning it to the left, and it just went right!"

J.B. sat up and dusted himself off. Morgan was already on his feet, and J.B., with Sonny hanging over him, suddenly felt like a man brought low by old age. He waved away Sonny's outstretched arm and hoisted himself up. His right side seemed paralyzed, until it began to throb.

"Honestly, J.B., I don't know what went wrong. I know how to run those suckers," he babbled, and J.B. was startled to see tears in the man's eyes.

"It's OK, I'm all right," he assured him, patting him on the shoulder. He glanced over at Morgan, Morgan of the interchangeable names, like an alias, who was eying Sonny with mild distaste. Morgan had saved his life.

"I guess that's it for tonight," Morgan said dryly, and walked past them.

"You're sure you're all right," Sonny persisted.

"Sure," said J.B., "don't worry about it," and he staggered manfully back to his trailer, where he fell, grunting, onto the bed. The pain, and his thoughts, kept sleep at arm's length.

Was Sonny a superb actor—or had that really been an accident? He couldn't wait around to find out.

Chapter 62

"You heard?"

"Yes," said Pandora, letting him in. "Last night at dinner. Are you all right, J.B.?"

He sank into the couch with a groan. "I guess I'll live—for a while."

"Turn around," she ordered, sitting down beside him. He moved sideways and she began kneading his shoulders and arms.

"Feels good," he acknowledged, ". . . even if your concern is a touch belated."

"I had things to do last night."

"Like what?"

"Make some phone calls . . . search some trailers."

He swung around and waited.

She rose and went to the kitchen. "Want some coffee? I was just making it when—."

"No!"

She returned with two cups and settled into the couch. He glared at her.

She had slipped away from dinner early, after hearing of the accident from Sonny and Morgan, and gone to search their trailers, beginning—and ending—with Sonny's.

"He has fifty thousand in cash stuffed inside a sock in his drawer."

"So," J.B. breathed, leaning back, "they paid him to kill me."

Pandora put down her cup and shook her head.

"I don't think so. They wouldn't have to pay him for doing his job—if it was his job. Even if they did want to give him a bonus, they wouldn't give him cash . . . they'd just send it to his bank, electronically."

She rose and paced the floor, fingering the collar of her robe.

"No, it had to be someone else who gave him the money."

"Wild Bill," J.B. blurted.

"Yes," she began, ". . . but he hadn't been on the missile range for months."

"So?" J.B. was becoming irritated. Who cared who had given Sonny the money? Someone wanted him dead, and Sonny, apparently, had been appointed executioner.

"If Wild Bill had wanted to kill you," Pandora continued, "he would have done it himself . . . as he tried to do later, in Cloudcroft. He could as easily have killed you here as sneaked into the compound to make a deal with Sonny."

Pandora pulled a curtain back and looked out at the mountains, ashy under the October sun. In the foreground, the workmen were scooping up the debris from the drilling. She let the curtain fall and turned to J.B.

"Do you know what I think? I think Wild Bill gave that money to Sonny to sabotage the laser."

J.B. thought for a moment. "Sonny did seem to have some acquaintance with computers. I remember hearing him talk about them with that boyfriend of yours."

Pandora grimaced and sat down on the couch. He looked away. "So you think Sonny was moonlighting."

"Yes."

"But if he's an agent, isn't he supposed to protect the project, make sure it goes as planned?"

"Well . . . yes and no," Pandora vacillated. "It would fit with what my friends told me."

"Those phone calls you made?" J.B. eased back into a corner of the couch, head back, eyes closed, as Pandora recounted how she had driven off the range to find a pay phone from which to call her friends. Sonny, they had informed her, was a protégé of the director of operations, who had opposed Straight Arrow from the start, preferring more direct action against Iran.

"To the point of sabotaging it?" J.B. asked, incredulous.

"Sonny was probably looking for opportunities . . . and Wild Bill presented him with one . . . along with a nice reward," she surmised.

"You mean we have one agency of government trying to undermine another?" He winced and lay back again.

Pandora nodded. "It happens."

"So it was that operations guy who wanted me dead," J.B. declared.

"I don't think he would have gone that far." Pandora hesitated. "I can't believe Arthur would have planned it."

"I never liked the way Arthur looked at me. Like one of those lizards that can snag you from three feet away with their long tongue." He sat up and peered into her face. "Anyway, why haven't I heard anything about my 'new identity?' He's had enough time to come up with something."

She had no answer. He pulled her around and down on the couch. She hesitated before kissing him briefly.

"We haven't had much time together lately."

"I've been . . . thinking," she mumbled.

He slipped his hand inside her robe. "What do you think?" he asked softly.

She tensed, and the recognition that she was already withdrawing pierced him. Then she relaxed and laid her head against his shoulder. A wisp of red hair fell against his lips.

"I haven't made the bed yet," she whispered. "Why don't we go back there?"

His touch was light, deliberate, slowly, oh so slowly arousing. She stroked him diffidently at first, then more surely. It was as if they were making love for the first time, instead of, possibly, the last.

Much later they lay cradled in each other's arms, quiet but wide awake. J.B. had not felt so relaxed in weeks, since their first night in Cloudcroft.

"What would you think of spending a couple of days in Cloudcroft again?" he asked.

She smiled. "I was just thinking of that night." Then she frowned.

"I don't imagine we'd have any more problems," he reassured her. "Tourist season is over."

She glanced at him. "We did miss the aspencade, didn't we? When do you want to go?"

"How about tomorrow?" He hoped his voice sounded casual.

She considered that for a moment. Then she raised her head to kiss him loudly on the cheek. "Why not!" she declared.

★ ★ ★

Was he using her? Of course. Did she know? Probably. But he was convinced there was only one way to leave White Sands alive, and that was by driving out with Pandora. He suspected that she was beginning to realize that, too. And if she happened to change her mind—. No, there was little chance of her going with him. He coughed to disperse the pang in his chest.

He went to the bathroom and took the gold bar from the toilet tank. He hefted it as he walked back to the bedroom. Not exactly the fortune he had dreamed of starting anew with, but nothing to sneeze at, either. Assuming it weighed about fifty pounds—. He reached for paper and a pencil to calculate. Fifty times sixteen ounces was eight hundred. The price of gold was maybe three hundred and fifty dollars an ounce. Christ, that was two hundred and eighty thousand dollars! That's a lot of tortillas and beans, old man, he grinned. Well, of course, no one was going to give him that much for a gold bar that came from God knew where. But if he got half of what it was worth, or even a third?

Now, how to take it out? He couldn't exactly stick it in his pocket. He would be taking an overnight bag to Cloudcroft. That was expected and natural. But he couldn't just carry the brick in the bag. What if he were searched at the border, or robbed?

As he pondered the problem, he began throwing things in the bag. Toothbrush, a couple of shirts, socks. He would need a jacket in the mountains. He slid a lined woolen jacket off its hanger and tossed it on the bed. He glanced at the boots on the floor of the closet. One pair was enough. Then he remembered. He picked up a boot and turned it over. The diamond-edged blade fell out. He picked it up and examined it. "Hmm," he grunted, stuffing it in his pants pocket.

He had dinner that night at the Club West. Sonny and Morgan were there, and the three drivers. Sonny apologized once again for almost burying J.B. in Straight Arrow's debris, but J.B. waved off with a smile his expressions of concern and self-reproach. The loader operator was less forgiving.

"Damn stupid," he spat. "You can hurt someone and wreck a good machine, too, if you don't know what you're doing."

The driver had come running out just after the incident and berated Sonny. Now Sonny scowled at him. He had had enough.

The others remained carefully neutral, and gratefully accepted bowls of green chile stew when dinner was served. Alfie did his best to lighten the conversation, but when there was no response, he retreated to the kitchen.

"I guess we'll go back to work tonight," Morgan drawled.

"What?" J.B. said, drawing a blank.

"We ought to finish pulling up Straight Arrow," he explained, glancing at the drivers, who were occupied with the stew.

J.B. took another bite before answering. He had had other plans for the evening. "Sure," he said, "you're right."

Sonny finished quickly, sopping up the last streaks of gravy with a piece of tortilla and popping it in his mouth. "I'm ready when you are," he announced.

J.B. rose slowly from the table. Was this trip necessary, he wondered? But of course it was. Mustn't let Sonny or Morgan get suspicious, and he'd already postponed pulling up the laser.

"Alfie!" he called. The cook appeared from the kitchen, and J.B. complimented him. "Alfie, that was the best damn chile stew I've ever had." Alfie beamed. "Thanks, J.B.," he said.

On impulse, J.B. went around the table to shake his hand. "You're a genius," he added warmly.

Alfie laughed. He hadn't heard such effusive praise since he had started cooking for the group. He watched J.B. walk out, pleased.

J.B. gave it three hours before he begged off on grounds of exhaustion. "My ribs feel like a Brahma bull's been dancing on them," he added.

Morgan grinned and Sonny looked sheepish. He waved to them both.

In his trailer, he sat at the kitchen table glaring at the bar of gold. Finally, he drew the diamond-edged saw from his pocket.

Hours later, he was rummaging through drawers and cupboards. Pandora was so thorough, surely she had stocked the place with needle and thread, at least one of those little traveling packets. He found a couple of them in the medicine chest.

Chapter 63

They left immediately after breakfast, J.B. yawning as he threw his bag into the back seat of the wagon and jumped in beside Pandora.

She raised her eyebrows as she shifted. "You have a long night?"

"Very," he sighed. "I get hooked on those old movies whenever I turn on the TV set."

The tires raked the dirt, and he turned with satisfaction to see Morgan and Sonny staring at them. They were too surprised to move, if they had a mind to, J.B. thought.

Down through the missile range they drove, the sun outlining Pandora's profile with flame. She glanced at him, uncomfortable with his long gaze, and he smiled and looked away, at the hills flattening out toward the west.

The guard at the gate recognized them, or her, and motioned them on. J.B. slumped down in the seat, exhaled a deep, tranquil breath, and drifted off. In his dreams, a monotonous buzz and clang, buzz and clang, receded down a darkening tunnel, while ahead, a dappled golden light expanded.

They were climbing when he woke, up into the Sacramento Mountains. Stands of aspen blazed among the somber pines, the last laugh of summer. In the open spaces, the startling, fragile purple of wild asters foretold the end of languid days and the harsh, unforgiving cold to come. It was a moment to savor, but Pandora interrupted it.

"You're terrific company," she remarked.

"I was hoarding my strength for our sojourn among the clouds."

They looked at each other and laughed.

They drove slowly through the streets of Cloudcroft, empty now of tourists and booths, and selected a lodge on the far side of the town that advertised individual cottages and cooking facilities. Pandora, remembering J.B.'s chagrin at their last outing, offered him a one-hundred-dollar bill before they left the wagon, then withdrew it. "No," she said, taking two more bills from her purse, "better take this." Their eyes met briefly as he accepted the bills, before she looked away.

"Well," he said, after they had dropped off their bags, "what would you like to do now?"

She shrugged. "Might as well see the aspens."

J.B. drove this time. Like the money in his pocket, it made him feel competent. After each curve in the road, a new wave of golden aspens hurled itself toward them. A squirrel darted into the narrow road and J.B. veered to avoid it, the wagon almost plummeting over the mountainside. The squirrel, naturally, had retreated. He backed up and drove on. The land leveled out and soon they were paralleling a tiny stream. The water was such a contrast to the dry desert of White Sands that J.B. pulled over.

Pandora hiked up her pants, pulled off boots and socks, and stumbled in over the rocks. "Come on in," she yelled back.

"Who, me? I'm a dryland cowboy," he protested.

Flailing her arms like a tightrope walker, Pandora waded upstream. She had pulled off the bandana that usually circled her head, and her hair unfurled in the breeze.

Damn, J.B. thought, with appreciation and regret. A goddamned CIA agent. She was as much a revelation to him as she had been that day some six months ago, when she kissed him in the visitors' room of the state pen. He longed to follow her into the stream. What held him back? He squatted at the edge and bravely poked a finger into the icy water. What held *her* back?

They drove on, passing an occasional house and a field of corn stubble, until the peak of Sierra Blanca rose above the pines and spruce and stared at them.

They returned to town slowly, silently. Stopping at a grocery store, they bought steaks, potatoes and salad makings, and a bottle of champagne, before returning to the lodge.

J.B. started a fire in the pit outside their cottage, then went looking for a bottle opener. He found an ancient corkscrew with which he deftly mutilated the cork before pushing it down into the bottle. He poured champagne into plastic glasses and they went outside to sit before the fire in aluminum chairs. The sun's last rays pierced the spruce, while beyond, a smear of red spread through the sky. Pandora turned back toward him and then caught sight of something behind him. She pointed. A hunter's moon, looking like a pot of curdled cream, popped up from behind the treetops and rose quickly and smoothly into the darkening east, as if motorized. J.B. moved his chair around and Pandora put one arm over his shoulder. They sipped and stared. A pinpoint of starlight appeared beside the moon in counterpoint. Then the chirp and rasp of insects brought them down to earth.

J.B. tidied the bed of coals and hid the potatoes, wrapped in foil, in them. A half hour later he put the steaks on the grill.

"I guess my job is to make the salad," Pandora pouted, rising.

"You *could* be a little more feminine than going around shooting at things," J.B. pointed out. She flinched as he jumped up to kiss her nose. "But I'll help."

They ate before the fire, thoughtfully, glancing occasionally at the moon that drew them into its aura. It was almost at its zenith when they shivered in the deepening chill and buried the last embers.

"I feel grubby," she whispered when they kissed.

"Good," he said, "let's take a bath."

There was no bathtub, but they made do with the tiny shower stall, soaping each other deliberately, careful not to miss any spots, alternately giggling and sighing.

In bed, they reached for each other eagerly. There was no hesitation now. It was sheer lust, tempered only by the desire to please and satisfy. Satisfy? J.B. felt this was a coupling that would last him a lifetime. As well it might have to.

They paused to drink champagne, to laugh. They shared memories now. Then he kissed her breast, or she caressed him, and once more they set the plastic glasses aside.

"I love you, J.B.," she said, before they drew apart to sleep.

"I love you, Pandora," he answered.

It was about four in the morning when he woke. Pandora, illumined by scraps of moonlight, breathed steadily. He raised the covers gingerly and slipped out of bed. He dressed slowly, careful not to rustle fabric, buttoning but not zipping his pants. He picked up his boots and bag and tiptoed to the door.

As he stopped to look at her, she rolled onto her side. He waited. The regular breathing continued. Sorry to run out on you like this, he thought. This isn't how I imagined I'd leave. There was no response. But, of course, with her head turned to the wall, he couldn't see the tears rolling down her face.

Shivering in front of the cottage, he pulled on the boots and zipped his pants, and put on the woolen jacket. Bag in hand, he walked out to the road and turned west.

Striding down the main street of Cloudcroft, he passed the tennis courts, eerily empty, the park where he and Pandora had eaten sausage and surprised the Nazi. Ten minutes later he rounded the bend that marked the far side of the town.

The trees loomed over him. He felt like the last man alive on earth. Or was it the first? A slight flutter in the brush to his right brought him to a stop, just in time to see the white flags of a doe and her young as they plunged back into the woods.

It was about fifteen miles to the highway where he could expect to be picked up by a semi. He was beginning to feel the weight now, but the road was downhill, and it pulled him along faster. The sky was thinning to gray. A few birds emitted tentative cheeps.

It began to drizzle, and he had forgotten to take his hat. He tried to scrunch down into the raised collar of his jacket. But the tang of pine in the air buoyed him. He felt young and cocky. As he came out of the tunnel, there was the plash of water. A rivulet plinked down the mountain wall on his left. He stopped at the lookout where the hills opened up, framing the basin below. At the horizon, clouds rode below the San Andres, almost touching the ground.

He frowned as he turned back to the road. What was the name of that character he had read about, the golden man the Spanish conquistadors, and a couple of Germans, too, had searched for in South America? Ah, yes, El Dorado. The Indians rolled him in gold when they elected him chief of the tribe. Well. J.B. was not exactly rolling in gold. But he could afford a few tortillas and maybe a hammock on some beach.

The smears of fog hanging in the trees, in the crotches of hills, began to dissipate. By the time he came out onto the highway, the sun was warming his back.

He wondered whether Pandora would get in trouble for having helped him escape—unknowingly or knowingly. And probably the latter. He dismissed the idea. She'd done her job, keeping him working on Straight Arrow. She hadn't been informed of the plan to double-cross him.

Had Sam known? He seemed to have suspected something. But no, Sam was too much enamored of people and their follies, not of any bureaucracy. He would have warned him outright.

Maybe there'd be a señorita on that beach—.

Air brakes whistled and sighed behind him. A truck was pulling over. The driver opened the door and called out. "I'm goin' to El Paso."

"Great!" J.B. responded. He threw the bag in and, with some effort, hoisted himself up into the cab. The driver looked him over casually as he put the truck in gear.

"You look pretty happy," the driver observed. J.B. realized he'd been smiling.

"I'm on my way home, to see my family," he explained. The driver nodded.

J.B. leaned back. Yes, on my way home. With all the gold I can carry sliced up and sewn into the lining of my jacket.

He accepted a cigarette from the driver and exhaled, watching the smoke swirl out the window and waft away toward White Sands.

Chapter 64

"We lost the laser, Mr. President."

"What?"

"Yes. It happened when we struck oil."

"What?" The president was annoyed. He was starting to sound like a sick duck. He folded his hands on the desk and closed his eyes. "Just tell us slowly and simply, Arthur," he directed his defense secretary, "what happened."

"I can't imagine how we missed it before." Arthur paused to look out the window at the Washington Monument. It never failed to stir his patriotic fervor. Or something that felt like it. "Apparently the laser slid right by it, just weakening the rock—or maybe there was a shift in the plates. At any rate, this time, when we brought the laser up to six thousand feet, the tunnel caved in, and the laser was swamped by the oil pouring in."

"How much oil is there?" Sam asked.

"Our geologists estimate the reservoir at six to seven hundred thousand barrels."

The president was incredulous. After this convoluted plan to rob Iran of its oil, they had found a bonanza in their own backyard.

"Of course, we stopped the flow immediately," Arthur continued. "We'll fill in the tunnel and no one—."

"What?" the president squawked.

"Well," Arthur explained patiently, "it seems that the operation was set up on what is actually a parcel of state land within the missile range. We've had it condemned, of course, as we have similar parcels, but the state of New Mexico has questioned our appraisal of the land—as they always do," he added significantly, suggesting obstructionism or a deficiency of loyalty. "It will be in the courts for some time."

He leaned over the desk of the president, who withdrew more deeply into his chair. "Naturally, Mr. President," he continued, "it would not do to let the state learn of the windfall that lies beneath that particular parcel."

Sam chuckled. "There's no end to our bamboozling that state, is there?"

Arthur straightened and went back to the window. "Of course, even if we owned the property, we would leave the oil in place."

"Why?" The president was relieved that Bob had asked the question. Now he waited for a fresh confirmation of his PR man's naïveté.

"We cannot have a horde of outsiders descending on a top-secret installation like the missile range. It's enough that we know the oil is there. It will be accessible in the event of an emergency."

"Well, the price of gas *is* stabilizing," Sam conceded. Arthur glanced at him. "At about twice what it was a year ago."

"What about—that man?" the president asked. "Did you take care of him?"

Arthur frowned. "It seems he chose not to wait for our aid, Mr. President. He left on his own, and has disappeared."

The president was tapping his pen on the desk. Truth to tell, he had never been too comfortable with Project Straight Arrow, and was relieved that it was ended.

"Too bad we couldn't do something for him," he said idly, his thoughts already moving on to other matters.

"Yes," Arthur agreed sincerely, "I regret that, too, Mr. President."